Ride Dirty

Also from Laura Kaye

Warrior Fight Club Series
FIGHTING FOR EVERYTHING (May 22, 2018)
FIGHTING FOR WHAT'S HIS (August 2018)
FIGHTING THE FIRE (October 2018)

Blasphemy Series
HARD TO SERVE
BOUND TO SUBMIT
MASTERING HER SENSES
EYES ON YOU
THEIRS TO TAKE
ON HIS KNEES

Raven Riders Series
RIDE HARD
RIDE ROUGH
RIDE WILD
RIDE WILD
RIDE DIRTY

Hard Ink Series
HARD AS IT GETS
HARD AS YOU CAN
HARD TO HOLD ON TO
HARD TO COME BY
HARD TO BE GOOD
HARD TO LET GO
HARD EVER AFTER
HARD AS STEEL
HARD EVER AFTER
HARD TO SERVE

Hearts in Darkness Duet
HEARTS IN DARKNESS
LOVE IN THE LIGHT

Heroes Series
HER FORBIDDEN HERO
ONE NIGHT WITH A HERO

Stand Alone Titles
DARE TO RESIST
JUST GOTTA SAY

Ride Dirty
A Raven Riders Novella

By Laura Kaye

1001 Dark Nights

EVIL EYE
CONCEPTS

Ride Dirty
A Raven Riders Novella
By Laura Kaye

1001 Dark Nights
Copyright 2018 Laura Kaye
ISBN: 978-1-948050-29-6

Foreword: Copyright 2014 M. J. Rose
Published by Evil Eye Concepts, Incorporated

Acknowledgments from the Author

This book, you guys. This book took me by surprise in so many ways. Caine McKannon had been an incredibly quiet character in my head before I started writing *Ride Dirty*, so I didn't know everything about his story until I was in the thick of it. He is one of my most tortured heroes ever, and writing his book was one of my most emotional experiences. I hope you love him as much as I adored writing him.

As always, I have a number of angels to thank for helping me bring this book to fruition. First and foremost, I must thank Liz Berry and the whole team at 1001 Dark Nights for the amazing support, above-and-beyond work, and incredible encouragement as I was writing this book. Working with Liz has been one of the highlights of my writing career, and I just feel so privileged to be able to do it.

I also have to thank my best friend, fellow author Lea Nolan, who was, as she always is, an amazing sounding board for the plotting and development of the story. I can always count on Lea to brainstorm with me and push me to figure things out, and I cherish her support so much.

Next, I absolutely have to thank the readers for having such amazing enthusiasm for another book in this series, which I have enjoyed writing so much. The Raven Riders are very alive in my head and I just love all the characters in this world so much. I appreciate all the readers who voted for this one last Raven Riders book and hope you'll think I gave Caine his due in *Ride Dirty*.

Special thanks to my Original Heroes and LKRG Facebook reader group for the constant excitement and support – you all make it all worthwhile!

Finally, thanks to *you* for taking my characters into your heart and allowing them to tell their stories again and again. ~LK

Sign up for the 1001 Dark Nights Newsletter
and be entered to win a Tiffany Key necklace.

There's a contest every month!

Go to www.1001DarkNights.com to subscribe.

As a bonus, all subscribers will receive a free copy of
Discovery Bundle Three
Featuring stories by
Sidney Bristol, Darcy Burke, T. Gephart
Stacey Kennedy, Adriana Locke
JB Salsbury, and Erika Wilde

One Thousand and One Dark Nights

Once upon a time, in the future...

*I was a student fascinated with stories and learning.
I studied philosophy, poetry, history, the occult, and
the art and science of love and magic. I had a vast
library at my father's home and collected thousands
of volumes of fantastic tales.*

*I learned all about ancient races and bygone
times. About myths and legends and dreams of all
people through the millennium. And the more I read
the stronger my imagination grew until I discovered
that I was able to travel into the stories... to actually
become part of them.*

*I wish I could say that I listened to my teacher
and respected my gift, as I ought to have. If I had, I
would not be telling you this tale now.
But I was foolhardy and confused, showing off
with bravery.*

*One afternoon, curious about the myth of the
Arabian Nights, I traveled back to ancient Persia to
see for myself if it was true that every day Shahryar
(Persian: شهريار, "king") married a new virgin, and then
sent yesterday's wife to be beheaded. It was written
and I had read, that by the time he met Scheherazade,
the vizier's daughter, he'd killed one thousand
women.*

*Something went wrong with my efforts. I arrived
in the midst of the story and somehow exchanged
places with Scheherazade — a phenomena that had
never occurred before and that still to this day, I
cannot explain.*

*Now I am trapped in that ancient past. I have
taken on Scheherazade's life and the only way I can
protect myself and stay alive is to do what she did to
protect herself and stay alive.*

*Every night the King calls for me and listens as I spin tales.
And when the evening ends and dawn breaks, I stop at a
point that leaves him breathless and yearning for more.
And so the King spares my life for one more day, so that
he might hear the rest of my dark tale.*

*As soon as I finish a story... I begin a new
one... like the one that you, dear reader, have before
you now.*

Dedication

To you,

"Pretty, pretty please, if you ever, ever feel like you're nothing
You're fuckin' perfect to me"

~ Pink

Chapter 1

Caine McKannon eased his naked body off the bed, doing his best not to disturb the couple entangled next to him. He retrieved his jeans from the floor and stepped into them, then repeated the process with his boots, shirt, hoodie, and leather-and-denim Raven Riders cut-off jacket. He'd shower the ménage off of his skin when he got home. Fucking he could always handle. Talking, not so much.

So it was time to fly.

Caine had perfected ghosting through his life before his age had hit double digits—silence had been a survival skill given the way he'd grown up—so he was surprised to find a pair of eyes on him when he turned. The man was older than him, early fifties maybe. Elliott was his name, not that it mattered. But he'd been the one to contact Caine about being a third with him and his wife through the message boards, one of the main ways he found partners who wouldn't have expectations for more.

Because Caine didn't do *more*. Not with women. Or men. Or even with the couples for whom he served as a twisted fucking fantasy fulfillment. Hell, Caine barely had friends, let alone anything more intimate. And he never had. Sometimes, he could hardly believe his brothers in the Raven Riders put up with his anti-social bullshit. Actually, calling him anti-social would've been *generous*.

But distance made him good at his job. Distance provided perspective, ensured dispassionate reasoning, kept everyone safe. Himself included. And that was his job for the club: Enforce the rules. Keep everyone safe.

Punish any sonofabitch who dared cross him or the club.

Tugging the black beanie down over his shorn hair, Caine gave the man in the bed a last look.

Elliott met his gaze and acknowledged him with a single nod, before pulling the sheet over his much younger wife's bare legs and ass like he was done sharing her. Caine had...absolutely no emotional reaction to the gesture at all. Sex wasn't about finding a place or making a connection. It was about getting off. Fulfilling a need. Scratching an itch. Finding a release. He'd been used and had used in return, and that was fine by him. But now, he'd fulfilled his purpose with these people, and they were as done with him as he was with them.

He left the McMansion like a whisper in the night and found his Dyna Fat Bob in front of the three-car garage. There wasn't any moon, so the bike was barely more than a shadow in the darkness. Working with one of his brothers who owned a custom chop shop, Caine had had the bike almost completely murdered out with a mix of black finishes that gave it a lean, brooding industrial feel, like it was more tactical weapon than motorcycle.

He got astride and heaved a sigh. It wasn't quite eleven and despite the sex, restlessness rattled through his veins, telling him sleep wouldn't find him any time soon. No sense going home. And he wasn't up for the Saturday-night partying no doubt going down at the clubhouse.

So he'd do what he always did when he couldn't sleep. Ride a circuit around town – swinging past the Ravens' big compound, the racetrack the club operated, his brothers' places, and the homes of the Ravens' protectees who weren't currently living in the cabins near their clubhouse. Patrolling wasn't something he was expected to do, or that anyone even knew he did. Just something that filled his time. Just a routine that gave him something to think about besides the lame-ass woe-is-me bullshit narrative that sometimes filled his head.

You're a fucking waste of space.

You're a worthless piece of shit.

You *should've been the one to die.*

Wah wah whatthefuckever.

His bike came to life on a low rolling growl, drowning out the ancient voices and the memories. He donned a matte black helmet and tugged a mouth mask up over his face, and then he was pulling out onto the street and making his way through town, past quiet homes and closed businesses. Glowing Christmas lights hung in trees and around rooflines and in darkened windows, not that the holiday meant anything to him.

Every time he made a left turn, his shifting weight reminded him that he'd been shot through the left wrist less than three months before. The memory of that night was part of the bullshit that pinballed around his skull—*not* because he'd been hurt, but because three others had been, too. And it was his fucking fault.

The only saving grace was that all three had survived, but clearly he needed to step up and do better watching over the members of the closest thing to a family he'd ever had. Because next time they might not be so lucky.

Nearly an hour into riding the circuit, Caine made his way into town to the row house of the last of their protectees, Ana Garcia. She'd been receiving death threats ever since filing a sexual assault charge against the pastor at a big church on the outskirts of town. One of those places that was as much fundraising machine as it was a house of worship. Powerful and connected, where the woman was not. Which was why she'd come to the Ravens, and why they'd agreed to take her on. It was what they did—protecting those who couldn't defend themselves, and it'd been the main thing that'd drawn Caine to the club ten years before.

He parked at the curb about a half block away from the client's house and cut his engine, content to keep eyes on the place for a while despite the December cold. The Ravens had offered to let her stay at one of their cabins, but she didn't want to be chased from her own house, so they'd been doing regular drive-bys and providing escorts around town, most recently during her courthouse appearance. The show of potential force was frequently enough to make the kind of cowardly shitheads who'd threaten a woman stand down, and so far that seemed to be the case for her.

On a sigh, Caine hung his helmet on the handle bar and got off the bike to walk the block. He moved like a shadow, quiet and quick, a black wraith in the night. Eyes wide open. Ears on alert. Instincts tuned to the tiniest threat. It was just how he was wired—or maybe it was how life had rewired him.

He was almost at the intersection across from their client's house when he heard it. A woman's shriek, abruptly cut off, quickly followed by the snarling, aggressive barks of a dog—and then a sharp yelp. *Not* from the direction of their protectee's place, but closer, from around the corner of the row houses right next to him.

Instincts screaming, Caine darted to the corner of the house closest to the intersection, his hand already at the small of his back…reaching for the gun he hadn't brought when his whole plan for the night had been the threesome. *Fuck.*

He peered around the corner and saw two people locked in physical struggle, a small dog barking and growling at their ankles. One person wore a mask, and the other a halo of long, blond hair.

Aw, hell no. He drew a switchblade from his boot and bolted toward them. He didn't speak, didn't wait, didn't hesitate. He popped the blade open and swung, catching the mask-wearing shitbag on the arm.

The guy hollered and reared back, suddenly off balance, the woman's purse in his hands as he went down on his ass. It was the perfect opportunity to pin him, except the woman lost her balance, too. She fell back against Caine's chest and, as he caught her, their feet became entangled in the dog's leash as the little thing jumped and yipped. It was all Caine could do to keep them upright.

And it allowed the attacker to recover. Her belongings spilling from the purse, he scrabbled off the ground and hauled ass up the street before disappearing down an alley.

"Sonofabitch," Caine growled, holding the woman by the shoulders as he tried to step out of the winding cord.

"Wait, wait," she said in a shaky voice. "Let me just unhook—"

"Be still," Caine said, frustrated as all hell that the man had gotten away.

"But—"

Finally, he got free of the leash, free of the heat of the woman against him, free of the dog scratching at the legs of his jeans. Bending down, the woman picked up the little puff ball and dropped the leash, allowing her to step out of the tangle, too.

She pressed her face to the thing's fur, her breath hitching. "Are you okay, baby?" The dog answered by licking her face, and then she ran her hands over its furry body. "Did he hurt you?"

Restless and agitated, Caine shifted feet. His gaze scanned the street, swung over all the shadowed places around them, took in the way the woman's wavy, sunny-blond hair spilled down over her long dark-blue coat. He folded and pocketed the knife. "You're the one you should be worried about."

Her gaze cut to him, allowing him to really see her for the first time.

Bright eyes the shade of the summer sky. Delicate features, almost stunningly pretty. A little gap between her two front teeth that added an endearing quality to all that pretty.

If Caine had been the type to find something endearing, which he wasn't.

She unleashed a shaky breath. "I...I can barely believe that just happened. Or that you helped me. Thank you."

He shook his head, not wanting the gratitude. Not when the man who'd jumped her had gotten away. "Why are you out alone at this hour anyway?"

Irritation replaced the gratitude in her gaze. "First of all, should that matter? Second, because dogs have to be walked—"

Her annoyance was easier for him to deal with. "At eleven at night?" he asked, suddenly angry that she'd seemed more concerned for her dog than her own safety.

"Wow. Okay." She rubbed a hand against her forehead as if he'd pained her. Turning away, she put the puff ball down and crouched to retrieve her scattered belongings from the cracked sidewalk. Pens, lipsticks, a package of mints. She reached for something farther away and a little moan spilled from her throat as she suddenly curled in on herself.

"What?" he asked, warily coming up beside her. "What's the matter?"

Hand against her forehead, she gave a little shake. "Nothing. I have a migraine. Was on my way back from the convenience store when he...he..." Another little shake, and she braced her free hand against the sidewalk. Whimpering, the puff ball tried to climb into her lap. "*That's* why I was out."

Fuck. Aren't I the asshole?

Always.

She unleashed a little laugh, but the sound was full of despair.

Caine gave the street another one-eighty scan, then crouched.

Those bright blues cut up to him. "Except now that guy has the medicine I just bought...along with my wallet and keys." She pressed her fingers into her forehead again. "Oh, God, what a mess."

Unsure what to say or do, Caine just watched her expressive face. Pain and unnamed emotion flickered across it, making him wish for just one moment that he was the kind of person who knew how to make things better.

On a sigh, she stuffed her loose belongings into her coat pocket. "Oh! I still have my phone." Her expression brightened as she pulled the device from her coat and stared at it like she'd won a prize. "I should call the police."

"They won't be able to help," he said.

She frowned and her shoulders fell. "You don't know that. And shouldn't I at least report it?"

Caine mentally kicked himself for dousing the little bit of happiness she'd latched onto in finding her phone, but he'd never been one for hiding from the truth. That only resulted in the truth finding you first. "Did you get a look at his face?"

Her gaze narrowed on him. "No, he wore a mask. You saw him, didn't you?"

He nodded. "And did anything else about his appearance strike you as noteworthy? Something the cops could use to identify him?"

"Oh." Her frown deepened, and then her eyes went wide. "You cut his arm."

"Not deep enough that he'll seek treatment," he said. At least, that's what Caine would've put his money on. Still, he had to give her credit for thinking of that detail.

"So then...I'm just out of luck." She stroked her hand over the brown, gray, and white little dog which now lay in a ball at her hip. "At least I still have you," she whispered as the puff ball raised its silly head. She looked so small sitting there, curled in on herself, head in her hand, but still able to find joy in the animal...

Out of nowhere, a memory surfaced. Of Grace, a few nights before the fire... Already at ten, Caine hadn't slept soundly, his body having of necessity developed a state of constant alertness he still possessed. So he'd often gotten up to check on his friends. Henry, who he shared a room with; Shawn, who was in the other boys' room; and little Grace, who'd taken to following Caine around from almost the first day she'd arrived, no matter how often he'd told her not to.

Grace hadn't been in her bed, and Caine had found her hiding in the closet of the girls' bedroom with a mangy white cat.

"Grace, you can't have that in here. You know if they find you—" His gut fell as he took in the bowl of milk. *If they realized someone had helped themselves...*

"I know," she said, six-year-old blue eyes peering up at him. "But he was on the fire escape, and he needs me. Isn't he cute?"

Caine sighed. "Stay off that fire escape. You know it's broken."

She stuck her tongue out at him. "I wasn't on *it. I just opened the window."*

Most of the other kids were too scared of Caine to talk to him at all, let alone to back-talk to him. Yet the littlest one of them all loved to give him a hard time. Resisting a smile, Caine had knelt down in the open doorway. "He is cute. But, Grace, you gotta look out for yourself first."

Petting the cat's rounded back, Grace shook her head. "That's not what you do, Caine. You always look out for me. Will you help me hide him?"

"Mister?"

The memory was like a punch to the gut. Caine sucked in a breath as the woman's voice pulled him out of it. "What?" he asked, rushing to his feet when he realized the blonde was standing over him, her little dog tucked against her chest.

Her gaze was wary. "I asked if you were okay."

A single shake, because his heart was jackrabbiting in his chest. Where the *fuck* had that memory come from? He hadn't thought of that night for *years*. "Yeah," he said, "but you're not."

And not just because of the migraine and the mugging, like those weren't enough. But the asshole had gotten away with her driver's license *and* her keys, a combination that had every one of Caine's internal alarms blaring.

She gave a little shrug. "It's over now," she said, taking a step away. "So thank you again. I'm gonna head home and call a locksmith."

He watched her, his instincts torn between helping and keeping out of something that wasn't his business.

Will you help me...?

Goddamnit, between the echo of Grace's long-ago plea still ringing in his ears and the fact that he'd let this woman's mugger get away, her plight now kinda was his fucking business, wasn't it? Whether he wanted it to be or not.

"So...okay, bye," she said, turning away altogether.

"Wait," Caine said, foreign words on the tip of his tongue. And then they were spilling free. "I can help you. With the locks. That is, if you want."

Chapter 2

Emma Kerry froze in her tracks, then turned to face the man who'd protected her. "How can you help with my locks?" she asked, her pulse pounding against the front of her skull. Given how this man had just helped her, part of her felt ashamed for feeling any wariness, but there was something about him that sent a chill down her spine.

He nailed her with a stare, his eyes startlingly pale blue, something that stood out when everything else about him was so dark. Black knit cap, black hoodie, black jeans, small black gauges in his ears, denim-and-black-leather cut-off jacket from that motorcycle club she sometimes saw around town. Patches on that jacket read:

Caine

Sgt. At Arms

Was Caine his first or last name? Or a nickname? She didn't know. But what she did know was that he was tall and possessed an edgy intensity that made her feel anxious. Or maybe that was just her projecting how on edge she felt after getting jumped.

"I know how to pick them," he said. "So I can let you into your house."

Hugging Chewy in tighter against her chest, Emma took an unconscious step backward. "Oh, uh, right." She gave a nervous laugh that sounded close to hysterical in her own ears. "Well, thanks, but I'll call a professional."

He shrugged. "Saturday night. They're gonna take hours."

Emma's instincts didn't know how to read this guy, because he made her feel both vulnerable and safe, like he was some kind of magnet that messed up her internal compass. It was probably this damn headache. "It's okay."

His brow slashed downward and he took a step closer. "Why won't you let me help?"

Her heart threatened to take flight, and she fell back another step as words rushed from her mouth. "Um. Because I don't know you. And you have a knife. And I just got mugged and now you're talking about breaking into my house?"

The man froze and held up his hands in a gesture of surrender. "Whoa. If I was going to hurt you, I could've done it by now."

Emma gasped, the truth of those words needling in even though... "That is not at *all* reassuring."

He winced, and it made him momentarily appear a little vulnerable himself. "I suck at reassuring."

"No kidding." Her stomach went on a loop-the-loop, because something about this man made her feel like she was standing on shaky ground.

Hands still raised, he took another step back. "I didn't mean to make it worse."

She shook her head, and the gesture made her feel a little nauseous. "You didn't. But I'm okay now. So, thank you." With that, she turned and rushed away. She would've sworn he watched her until she disappeared around the corner, and then she moved even faster just in case he followed. Thank God her place was only six houses down.

Except, of course, that she couldn't get in. Still, the golden glow of her front porch light and the colored lights on her Christmas tree that twinkled from her front window restored some of her sense of security. "Here you go, baby," she said, sitting on her stoop and settling her Shih Tzu in her lap. "I'm gonna get us in."

Her phone was her one saving grace of the whole night, and she used it to look up emergency lock-out services...only to find that the Caine guy was right. They gave her an estimate of ninety minutes. Which would put them here after midnight. Awesome.

Emma dropped her head into her hand. "If I throw up, I promise not to do it on you, Chewy."

The little guy spun in her lap, seemingly knowing she needed his comfort judging by how he nuzzled her face. She laughed at his antics despite herself.

She tugged the collar of her coat up around her neck and pulled her free hand inside her sleeves. With the other, she opened her e-reader app on her phone and found a new book to start. There was nothing to be done but wait. And the light of the app made her feel less alone.

She wasn't sure how much time had passed when the rev of a motorcycle engine tore into the quiet somewhere down the block, and both she and Chewy startled. The dog growled and ruffed out little half barks that expressed concern but not outright alarm. But then the motorcycle came toward them and its rumbling engine echoed louder off the buildings, sending Chewy into full-on protective mode.

Especially when the bike pulled to the empty curb in front of the house next to hers.

Caine. His boots braced against the ground as the sleek all-black Harley came to a stop.

Emma stared. Once again, her brain seemed to be caught in an internal war between fear and fascination, panic and relief. Definitely relief, if she wanted to be honest with herself.

The engine went dead, and silence rang loud in its wake.

"How long?" he called out.

She hesitated only a moment before realizing what he meant. "Til the locksmith?" Her phone said fifteen minutes had passed since she'd called. "About seventy-five minutes."

"Okay." Parked at the edge of the illumination cast by her lights, Emma could just make out Caine's movements. He crossed his arms and his head fell forward.

"Um, Caine?" she said, testing out that name.

"Yeah?"

She leaned forward to try to see him better. "What are you doing?"

A sigh that sounded like pure frustration. "Waiting."

"For?"

"You to be safe."

Those four words. Those four words added a *serious* dose of fascination to the relief his presence brought. Because why would he go to this trouble for her when he'd already helped her *and* she'd kinda brushed him off? Who did that?

But if she'd been blown away by his presence and his determination to watch out for her and those words, it was nothing compared to what happened next. About ten minutes later, Emma became aware of the distant sound of another motorcycle, but didn't think about it until it got closer—and then turned onto her street.

Somehow she knew it was going to stop near Caine, and then it did just that.

Emma felt like she was watching a movie and had absolutely no idea what was going to happen next. New biker guy handed Caine something, looked her way, and seemed to hold a conversation she couldn't quite hear over his motor. Then, as quickly as he came, he left again. Until the street was once more quiet and his engine noise became a distant whine.

Caine got off his bike, and Emma's pulse kicked up in her veins. She had no idea what was coming at her. And then he was in front of her, standing within the circle of light so that she could see him clearly. Her breath caught as those eyes landed on her. Ice-blue heat in a harsh face.   Harsh   all   except   for—

"Here," he said, holding something out to her.

—the soft fullness of his lips. Emma had to drag her gaze away to see what was in his hand. A plastic grocery bag swung heavy in his grip.

"What is it?" she asked.

One thick, dark brow arched upward toward the knit cap.

Chewy sniffed and danced in her lap, his tail wagging. Guess he'd made his vote on Caine clear.

Unleashing a shaky breath, she took the bag.

The moment she did, Caine stepped back into the shadows and returned to his bike. Only then did she peer into the bag.

Her heart was a sudden bass beat in her chest. She pulled out a bottle of water. A bottle of Coke. And bottles of Excedrin, Aleve, and aspirin. Chewy sniffed each item as she pulled it out.

Emma could only stare at the small pharmacy she lined up on the stoop next to her. He'd...called someone to get her medicine? And they'd actually gone and bought it and then drove it to him—for her?

Who. Did. That?

"Is it...the right stuff?" he asked quietly, his voice coming to her from the darkness.

Seriously. No one did that. Who was this guy?

"I can't believe you did this," she said.

"Fuck. It's *not* the right stuff?"

She shook away the disbelief. "No, no. It is. Thank you. I'm just...stunned."

And totally not willing to look a gift horse in the mouth. Not when this night had unleashed a marching band in her head—and that had been true *before* getting mugged, getting saved by a biker, and then...getting saved by him again?

She uncapped the Excedrin and the Aleve, fought through the foil seals and stuffed cotton balls, and greedily swallowed down two pills of each medicine with a long gulp of the Coke.

"I'll pay you back as soon as I can," she said, grateful beyond words. It'd been a long time since anyone had looked out for her like this. Not since the grandmother who'd raised her died three years ago.

He didn't respond, and she had the strangest feeling that she'd said the wrong thing.

Emma debated. Resisted. Debated again. Then sat Chewy on her stoop and pointed at him with a "Stay." Her stomach flipped as she stepped down to the sidewalk. But there was still that relief and even more of that fascination, and so she approached his bike like he was a lion who was maybe wild and would eat her alive but maybe, just maybe, tame and would let her pet him. Which was a totally weird way to think of a man, but whatever, it seemed right here. For *this* man.

Even though she couldn't make out his face in the shadows, she felt his eyes on her almost immediately. Emma fisted her hands at her sides and forced her feet to keep moving until she reached the edge of the sidewalk just a few feet from his bike. From him.

"Thank you," she said.

He palmed the cap on his head. "You said that already."

His gruffness might've hurt her feelings if she hadn't gotten the feeling that her gratitude made him uncomfortable. "Well, all of this is worth saying it more than once."

He breathed out heavily from his nose, a sound of exhaustion...or exasperation. Emma didn't know.

She stuffed her hands in her pockets. "You don't have to stay, you know. I'll be okay. Especially after the medicine."

He crossed his arms. "I'm staying."

"Why?"

"You *want* me to go?"

"*No*," she rushed out, stepping down off the curb. Closer to him. Close enough that she caught the flash of his eyes in the dimness. "No, I don't. I just don't know why you're going to such lengths to help me.

That's all. Curiosity."

"Curiosity killed the…"

"…the cat. Yeah, yeah, I walked into that one, didn't I?" She chuckled. "Seriously, though."

"I let him get away."

"What?"

Now his sigh was more like a growl. "The asshole who jumped you. I let him get away."

Wait. He felt guilty? "You didn't *let* him—"

"I did. And now he has your keys and your address. And you're stuck outside in the freezing cold at midnight."

A chill raced down Emma's spine. Because in the midst of everything else, she hadn't put those two facts together in quite that way. For just a moment, her headache fought back against the pain meds. "Do you think he'll come back?"

"Fuck," he bit out. "I didn't mean to…probably not, okay? Guy was probably just a junkie hoping for some cash for his next fix."

Emma wasn't sure that made her feel much better. Because her purse was still going to be floating around out there…somewhere. And not just with her keys and license, but with all her credit cards, too. Canceling those was one more thing she needed to do once she was done with the locksmith. "You're probably right," she managed. And then, with more conviction, "None of which is your fault, obviously."

"*Look, lady—*"

"Emma."

"What?"

"My name is Emma. And I'm totally not old enough for you to call me *lady*."

He huffed, and she could almost hear him roll his eyes.

She found herself biting back a smile. "You sigh a lot."

"You talk a lot."

That made her laugh. "I know. Hazard of my job, I guess."

He shifted on his bike, and his boot scuffed the pavement. "Which is?"

She almost missed the question, but her belly gave a weird little flip that he'd asked. He didn't seem like a jobs-and-weather small-talk kinda guy. "I teach kindergarten. When you spend your days with twenty-three five- and six-year-olds, you're bound to be talkative."

He grimaced and scrubbed a hand over his face.

Now she was the one sighing. Because she felt like she'd said something wrong again.

Which made her want to do something that might help him. And, in a weird way, allowing him to help her actually would help him, too. Because then he wouldn't have to sit here anymore either. In the freezing cold at midnight.

So she swallowed down the little ball of nerves suddenly in her throat and asked, "Still want to pick my lock?"

His head jerked toward her and then he was off the bike and standing right in front of her.

And wow if all that intensity wasn't overwhelming up close. Overwhelming and strangely breathtaking. "Is that a yes?" she whispered.

"Hell, yes."

Chapter 3

It took Caine less than a minute to let Emma into her house. She gawped as he pushed the door open and gestured for her to go in. Chewy raced ahead, his nails clicking against the hard woods.

Emma cleared her throat. "That was impressive. And kinda scary. Are you that good or is my lock that weak?"

"Both," he said, pocketing the key ring that held the little wire devices he'd used.

"Well, that's, er, not really..." She swallowed the words, not wanting to criticize him again.

But he apparently heard it anyway. "I suck at reassuring, remember?"

She shook her head. "No, it's just that... I don't know, maybe it's better not to hide from the truth anyway?"

His gaze collided with hers, and there was an intensity there she didn't understand. One that made her pulse race with a new dose of that fascination. "Always."

Nodding, she stepped into her entryway and peered at Caine. She wanted to thank him—again—but didn't think he'd appreciate it given their earlier conversation. So instead she smiled and said, "You were my hero tonight, Caine."

"Never call me that," he bit out, those icy blue eyes narrowed to slits.

Emma's heart tripped over itself and her tongue got tangled. And then it didn't matter that she didn't know how to respond because he was off her stoop in a flash. Back into the shadows and on his bike.

Er, that...had *not* gone the way she intended.

Stomach falling, Emma debated, but this time she erred on the side of leaving him alone. On a tired exhale, she closed her front door and nearly moaned from how good it felt to be inside where it was warm. She shrugged out of her coat and hung it in the front closet, and then leaned against the door jamb to her living room and admired the colorful glow of the lights on her tree—the only lights she had on.

She adored sitting in a room lit only by her Christmas tree. It was something she'd picked up from her grandmother, who used to spread a blanket out on this very floor in front of the tree and tell Emma stories—made-up stories about fantastical worlds, or real-life stories about when Emma's mother had been young. Stories her mother hadn't been around long enough to tell herself because a pulmonary embolism had taken her away when Emma had been just nine.

Still, Emma didn't associate the warm, almost magical glow of the lights with sadness. Instead, they made her feel closer to the women she'd loved and lost—which was why she was firmly part of the camp that put up decorations the day after Thanksgiving—tree, lights, and her grandmother's Santa collection, too—and didn't feel the slightest bit self-conscious if they stayed up well into the latter part of January.

Heck, she'd been the proud owner of a Valentine's tree or two.

She grinned at where Chewy had curled up in his plush dog bed, his well-groomed little head resting on a stuffed Chewbacca. His namesake. As a girl, Emma had thought the expressive sounds that the Star Wars character made were the cutest things she'd ever heard. And when she'd adopted the little guy the summer before she started her job at Frederick Elementary, she'd still remembered that. "You have a hard life, you know that?"

In answer, the dog gave a big sigh and burrowed in deeper.

And the sigh made her realize…she hadn't heard a motorcycle engine start up.

Frowning, she went to her front window and peered around the tree. Sure enough, Caine's dark silhouette remained. Part man, part motorcycle. As if he were some sort of mythical creature from her grandmother's stories.

Why hadn't he left…?

Her gut gave her the answer that, holy crap, he was waiting. Because even though he'd gotten her inside out of the cold and made sure she had medicine, her locks weren't yet changed and her keys were still out there somewhere…which meant Caine wasn't going to leave.

A tingle ran down her spine.

"This isn't right," she said. The man had saved her. Taken care of her. The least she could do was invite him in to wait. Determined, she marched to her door and went back out onto the stoop. "You're still waiting." He didn't answer. "Obviously, you're still waiting. So, come in."

That got a reply. "What?"

"Come in already. It's cold out here." She hugged herself.

"Good night, Emma."

She made for his bike. "This is ridiculous. If you're going to insist on waiting, which is very much above and beyond, then I have to insist on you doing it inside my house where it's not freezing."

Arms crossed, his voice was a low rumble. "You have to insist?"

Two could play the stubborn game. And she dealt with five-year-olds for a living, so he didn't know who he was dealing with. She crossed her arms, too. "I do."

He tilted his face toward her, allowing her to just make out the stern set of his features. And it was the first time that all that edgy intensity, all that darkness, and all that gruffness tripped the switch in her brain that registered sex appeal. Registered it *hard*.

This guy was nothing like the men she occasionally dated—other young professionals she met at her gym or through friends. But, man, there was something about this dark knight thing Caine had going on that was suddenly—and epically—hot. Maybe it was the way his long legs stretched out from the bike. Or the way his crossed arms emphasized the breadth of his shoulders. Or the way seeing him in shadow emphasized the strong angles of his face.

"What happened to my being a stranger and having a knife and breaking into your house?" he asked.

She almost laughed because he was so obvious in his attempt to be not-reassuring now. Which, go figure, actually *was* reassuring. "Well, in the time since you used your knife to protect me, we've gotten on a first-name basis, you had someone bring me medicine, and you used your powers for good. Plus Chewy wagged his tail at you and he's a very good judge of character. So…" She gestured toward her house and grinned. "Won't you please come in?"

* * * *

This is not a good fucking idea.

That was Caine's thought as he dismounted the bike.

So then why was he doing it?

It had better not be because the blonde was cute as fuck. Though she was. And not just because she was pretty. She was also playful and talkative, earnest and funny. And she didn't seem put off by him, even when he tried to put her off. All of that reminded him of someone he once knew. Someone who'd once been stuck to him like glue no matter what he'd said. Someone who'd once called him her hero.

Someone he didn't want to be reminded of.

So, yeah, it had better not be because of any of *that.*

As he climbed the steps to her row house, he felt like he was headed to the goddamned gallows. Which just proved how big of a fucking misfit he was.

"If they're true to their estimate, it should only be another thirty minutes," she said as she led him into the living room.

A place where, apparently, Santa Claus knickknacks went to die judging by the sheer number of them. Jesus. He peered around. Big, little, glass, wooden…Santas appeared on every surface. The mantle. The end tables. The built-in bookcase. Behind him, a big tree blocked most of the front windows, its branches laden with colored lights and ornaments. But even if Christmas hadn't thrown up all over her living room, the place would've appeared feminine, what with the overstuffed white furniture, baby blue pillows, and frilly lamps and floral curtains.

"Go ahead, make your comment," she said from behind him.

He turned to find her in the doorway that led to the dining room and kitchen beyond. The light of which backlit her hair, making it glow in a halo around her face.

Like he needed the reminder of her sweetness and decency. She was a kindergarten teacher, for God's sake, which nearly made her the poster child for wholesome innocence. And he'd had a threesome with strangers earlier tonight. Caine shook his head. What the hell was he doing in her house again? "Nothing to say."

She arched a brow, seemingly unaware of how out of place he felt. He was the guy best left in the shadows to rain down justice when it needed to be dispensed—the ache in his not fully healed hand was just the most recent reminder of that. He wasn't the guy you made nice with and invited inside. And never had been.

"Really?" she teased.

"A wise man knows when to keep silent."

She laughed. "Does a wise man also like coffee? Soda?"

"I don't need anything." Standing in the middle of the living room, he literally itched to leave. "In fact, I'm just gonna—"

"Oh, come on. Don't make me eat Christmas cookies at midnight by myself." She waved for him to follow as she turned toward the back of the house.

His stomach clenched, cementing his feet in place. When had he last eaten? The apple at breakfast?

Emma stopped in her kitchen doorway. "You coming?"

Without the bulk of the winter coat surrounding her, the slight build of her frame was more visible, even in the jeans and oversized sweatshirt she wore. He'd thought her features delicate, but in truth, all of her appeared that way, and it soured his gut to remember how she'd been struggling with her mugger when he'd first come upon them.

Warily, he followed her into the kitchen, a small but bright room with yellow walls, white cabinets, and a two-seater table. Besides two Christmas placemats on the table, the holiday hadn't vomited in here, and it made Caine feel slightly less on edge. He didn't hold anyone's love of the season against them, but for him the day had only ever represented disappointment and all the things he didn't have. And never would.

Arms crossed, Caine stood near the doorway and watched Emma as she washed her hands and retrieved a canister and napkins.

"Okay, coffee or soda? Or water? Or tea?" She smiled. "Basically anything except alcohol which I sadly have none of at the moment."

"Water's fine," he said, not at all surprised she didn't have alcohol in her house. Not that he cared. He drank only infrequently, not liking the feeling of his senses being dulled, or his reaction time being delayed. But it was just another little confirmation of her wholesomeness that was so unlike himself.

"You sure?" She opened her refrigerator door covered in kids' stick-figure drawings and peered in. "I have milk, too."

Shaking his head, he was about to reiterate his choice when his gaze landed on something in her fridge and his eyes went wide. "Is that orange soda?"

She grabbed two and grinned. "It *is* orange soda. You like?"

He shrugged with one shoulder. He hadn't had an orange soda in years, but once upon a time it'd been a childhood favorite. One of the few treats the home offered the kids.

Emma put ice in glasses and placed the drinks on the table. "Sit down. I'll bring the cookies over."

"Mind if I wash my hands first?" he asked. The longer he spent in Emma's presence, the more he felt the ménage clinging to his skin, and it was nauseating. Or maybe that was a side effect of his hunger.

"Of course."

When he was done, he sat on the edge of the closest seat and popped open his can. Bubbles fizzed over his fingers, and the sweetness of orange hit his nose as he poured.

"Okay, there's snickerdoodles, chocolate chip, molasses, peanut butter, and sugar cookies. I can take credit for everything except the peanut butter," Emma said. "They always turn out too dry when I make them. And then I discovered the ones at Dutch's and they're *amazing*, so those I bought. I think they got a new baker in there because they've seriously upped their dessert game. Do you know that place?" Emma brought a heaping plate of cookies to the table and slid into the other chair.

Small talk normally wasn't his strong suit—he never saw the point. But this was actually a topic he knew something about. "Yeah, the club hangs at Dutch's," he said, referring to a nearby diner whose owner had always been friendly to the Ravens. "And her name's Haven."

Pouring her drink, Emma placed three cookies onto a napkin in front of her. "Who?"

He took an iced snow man. "Dutch's new baker. She's the club president's girlfriend." Well, fiancée now. Caine had been present with the rest of the club when Dare Kenyon had gotten down on one knee and proposed to Haven at Thanksgiving dinner. He wasn't the only one who'd paired off during the last year, but he was the one who surprised Caine the most. He'd always thought Dare too married to the club to ever make room for anything more than hook-ups. Caine definitely felt that way. Which was convenient since he never let himself get close enough to anyone to chance feeling or wanting more.

He'd learned the hard way that it was a chance not worth taking.

People couldn't hurt you as much if you didn't care about them.

"No way! You *know* her?" Emma's eyes went wide, her gaze full of what looked like awe and delight. Two emotions rarely directed at him, that was for fucking sure.

And it hit him funny, almost like the scary thrill of nearly taking a turn too fast and too tight on his bike.

Caine nodded as he finished the first cookie. And it was like that first one emphasized how empty his stomach was, because he was suddenly ravenous. "That was good. You mind?" He gestured toward the plate.

"No, of course not. Have as many as you want."

He took a chocolate chip and then glanced up at Emma again.

To find her eyeballing his Ravens cut. "What's it like to be in a motorcycle club?" Her eyes went wide. "Is that too personal to ask?"

Maybe? Eyeballing her right back, he chewed and swallowed. Debated. And then settled on the most important thing, to him. "It's like having a big family. One you can actually count on." Unlike the one he'd been born into.

"A big family that brings you medicine to give to a strange lady just because you ask?"

His gaze dropped as he finished his cookie. After Emma had left him standing on the street, Caine had searched the alley down which her mugger had escaped, and then looped around the block to his bike— which was when he'd seen Emma sitting on her stoop and made up his mind to hang until she was safe. He'd called the Ravens' newest prospective member to run the meds errand for him. Because that was the shit that Prospects did. And because Caine hadn't liked seeing Emma curled up on the sidewalk in pain.

Not that he really wanted to revisit any of that with her.

"Pretty much. Not what you expected?" he asked, ready to hear the judgment or see the wariness or disapproval he so often encountered among strangers when it came to the club. He didn't give it any weight anymore, but that didn't mean he didn't see it happening around him.

Her expression went thoughtful. "I'm not sure what I expected. But what you described sounds awesome."

Her honesty impressed him, and so did the way she'd listened to him and seemed to consider what he had to say. His brothers gave him that kind of respect, but it wasn't something he'd found a lot of in his life. And though he appreciated it from her, it also left him feeling strangely…vulnerable. As if her sincerity and open-mindedness were picks that might open the locks inside him. So he changed the subject—and the tenor of the conversation. "Anyway, I thought you weren't old enough to be called *lady*?"

She laughed, and it made those sky blues shine with amusement. Also not something usually directed his way. Shit, he'd known Haven for seven months—and he liked her as well as he liked anyone—and she *still* approached him like he was a stray dog who might take her hand off. And that was no shade on Haven, either. Caine absolutely had the disposition of a distrusting stray who'd been abused enough to bite even the kindest hands.

"Touché," she said, brushing cookie crumbs off her fingers onto a napkin. "These cookies are making me realize I never ate dinner. Was too nauseous earlier."

"But you're not now?" he asked, taking a third cookie. A peanut butter, this time, because Dare always hoarded all the PBs when Haven made them for the club, meaning no one else ever got any. And, weirdly, eating was making him realize how hungry he was, too.

"No, the pills and the caffeine helped. I'd thank you again except I don't think you'd want me to." She arched a brow. Caine wasn't sure which gave him more satisfaction—that he'd helped her or that she seemed to be flirting with him.

He just looked at her, amused by the way she tried to get under his skin but unwilling to show it. And also not willing to examine too closely the fact that she was successful.

A slow smile grew on her pretty face, but she switched topics. "You want a sandwich?"

Caine blinked. His gut growled. Out loud. "No."

She laughed at him. "I think your stomach disagrees." She crossed to her fridge again, and the mass of kids' drawings fluttered as she opened the door. "I have ham and a couple kinds of cheese, which I could do cold or grilled. And I have a rotisserie chicken I could cut up."

"Emma—"

"What?" She peered over her shoulder.

The dog came trotting into the room and sat down close to the fridge.

"This is because I said 'cheese' out loud." She smiled down at the puff ball. "Isn't it, Chewy? You're crazy for cheese, aren't you?"

"Chewy?"

"Short for Chewbacca."

Caine frowned, unsure why he kept asking for these little details about her life but seemingly unable to stop himself. "The giant Star Wars character?"

"Yup." She crouched down to pet the little round head. "Because Wookiees are awesome. Now, sandwich?"

Knock, knock, knock.

Chewy took off at a tear, barking his not-at-all threatening head off.

"Aw, well, I guess we'll hold that thought for now," Emma said, her tone disappointed.

But the weirdest thing was that Caine was disappointed, too. Because once her locks had been replaced, he'd have absolutely no reason to stay.

Chapter 4

Despite the fact that it was eight days til Christmas, Monday morning was mild enough for Emma to walk the twenty minutes through downtown to Frederick Elementary School. She'd been excited about that when she first realized it was in the mid-forties, because the closeness of her grandmother's house—*her* house, now—to work was one of the many reasons Emma loved living there. But then her thoughts had resurrected what'd happened Saturday night.

The man jumping out of the bushes. Grabbing her. Pushing his body against her. Kicking her dog as his grip on her wrist tightened.

The flashes of those memories had come at her all weekend, distracting her, making her nervous, keeping her awake.

And almost making her drive to school.

Screw that, she thought as she passed the convenience store that marked the halfway point of her walk. She was not going to allow fear to rule her life. At least, not as much as she could help it. So, she'd walked.

Without question, Caine had helped make her less fearful, too. Because while the locksmith had changed out the locks on her front and back doors, Caine had shared that he worked in security, and asked if she wanted him to check out her place for other things she might do to secure it.

Remembering how easily he'd picked the lock to her front door, she'd agreed. He'd methodically gone through her first floor evaluating her doors and windows, and then examined her back porch and the basement door, too. She'd been disappointed when the locksmith's arrival had interrupted getting to talk more to Caine over a meal, but watching him move through her space had *not* been a hardship. He just had an intensity about him that was compelling. Maybe it was the way those strange pale eyes narrowed in cold calculation. Or maybe it was the almost stealthy way he moved, like a big cat that was at once both graceful and lethal. Or maybe it was the slivers of tattoos that his movements had revealed on his neck and side. All she knew was that she was fascinated. And curious. And, if her nighttime thoughts were any indication, more than a little lustful...

When he'd finished looking everything over that night, Emma became the proud owner of three new jimmy-proof deadbolts and spring-loaded security bars on the three first-floor windows that could be reached from the ground or back porch.

Except then Caine had left. He'd turned down her invitation to stay to eat, saying only, "Remember, Emma, you gotta look out for yourself first."

Crossing the last intersection before entering school grounds, Emma sighed. Because she hadn't been brave enough in that moment to ask for his phone number. So now she didn't know how to get ahold of him, and suspected he wouldn't want her to, anyway.

Thankfully, she'd soon have twenty-three really good distractions from *all* of that. Because nothing put her in a better mood or helped her gain perspective better than her kids.

Inside, the building was still quiet. Because she hadn't been able to sleep, she'd gotten ready earlier than usual. But at least she'd get a head start on the day. She'd have about forty-five minutes before the kids started arriving, which would be just enough time to set up all the art supplies for the holiday crafts she was having them start on today. Pom-pom Christmas trees, snowmen, and menorahs. Little presents for their parents. Because nothing said festive like fuzzy pom-poms!

"Good morning, Connie," she called, leaning into the principal's office.

"Morning, Emma. Getting a jump on the week?" Connie was the school's often miracle-working office manager, and Emma really liked the older lady. But she *hated* how the word "jump" brought more of those little flashes of memory.

"Yep," Emma said. "One more week."

Connie laughed. "Hang in there."

Grinning, Emma nodded. It was the last week of school before winter break, and without question, the kids would be bouncing off the walls by Friday. "You, too." A few of the other teachers were also in early, and Emma called out more greetings as she moved through school to the kindergarten hallway, where four kindergarten classrooms shared a wing at the back of the building.

Flicking on her classroom lights, Emma made for her desk. She frowned.

The room was unusually chilly.

And then she froze in place.

Papers and books were scattered across the floor near her desk...the top of which was all disorganized. Her gaze tracked to the left, where broken glass littered the top shelf of the low bookcases under the windows.

The window above was broken. A cobweb of cracks formed outward from a hole in the center of one of the big rectangular panes.

Emma's heart tripped into a sprint. She moved closer and saw what had made the hole.

A brick lay in pieces on the tile floor amid a trail of broken glass and strewn papers.

"Holy shit," Emma whispered. "What the hell?"

Disbelievingly, she dumped her coat and purse onto the nearest table. And then she made for the intercom box on the wall by the back door. She pressed the button. "Connie, it's Emma. Is Principal Mackey in yet?"

"She just arrived. Is everything okay?"

"No. My room... There's been vandalism. Someone threw a brick through the window." Emma wondered if the shakiness in her voice carried through the intercom.

"Oh, my goodness. We'll be right there."

True to her word, Connie and Principal Mackey arrived in under three minutes, mirror expressions of concern on their faces.

Wearing a smart pantsuit, the principal shook her head as she took in the damage. "Well, this isn't the way to start off a Monday morning, is it?"

"No," Emma said, still a little stunned. And man if she wasn't having a streak of bad luck lately. "No, it's not."

"All right," the principal said. "Connie, can you get Mr. Wilkerson in here to clean up and do what he can to cover the window? And I'll call the police. They won't be able to do much, of course, but I'll need them to file the report."

Her words reminded Emma of what Caine had said about reporting her mugger, and it set off a sharp pang in her chest. Of helplessness—and of anger, too.

"I'll get Mr. Wilkerson right now," Connie said, threading her way back through the classroom. "I'm so sorry, Emma."

She nodded and hugged herself against the chill in the air. "Thanks."

Principal Mackey placed a manicured brown hand on her arm. "You okay?"

"Yeah, yes. Of course. Just surprised. And worried that it might upset the kids." Emma supposed there was a teachable moment in this mess somewhere. Maybe she could use it as a good segue for talking to the students about the importance of caring for property that belongs to another person or the school. "I should email the parents to let them know in case the kids come home with questions." Entirely likely, since kids this age were little question machines.

Principal Mackey nodded. "Maybe we can get the school resource officer to come over from the high school and pop in to say hi to the classes." All the high schools in the county had an SRO, and the middle schools shared two officers, but the elementary schools didn't have them yet.

"That might be good, too," Emma said just as the janitor arrived, pushing a cart of tools and supplies. "Oh, good morning, Mr. Wilkerson."

"Miss Kerry, Principal Mackey," he said, his gaze going to the window. "I'll get this all fixed right up."

"Thank you," Emma said. She blew out a long breath, needing to shake off the adrenaline running through her veins before the kids arrived. She didn't want to do anything or behave in any way that might make them worry, and children were incredibly intuitive and empathetic.

Mr. Wilkerson made for the window, then stared up at it with his hands on his hips. "Mind if I move these books and bins so I can stand on this shelf?"

"Oh, no. Of course not. Let me clear some space," she said, crossing the room.

The man shook his head. "No, ma'am. Everything's covered with glass. I wouldn't want you to get cut."

She smiled. He always called her "ma'am" even though he couldn't have been that much older than her twenty-seven, and that made her think of teasing Caine about calling her *lady*. But as Mr. Wilkerson cleared away her things and climbed up on the bookcase, Emma didn't have time to think of the intriguing mystery that was her savior from the other night. Instead, she watched as Mr. Wilkerson cut a piece of plastic off a roll and began to duct tape a rectangle over the breach.

He was new this school year, and in addition to the attention he paid to his janitorial duties, he'd taken on a number of handyman projects around the school that everyone appreciated. Repairing a section of ductwork to the heating and cooling system that improved climate control in the whole kindergarten wing. Fixing windows around the school that didn't close securely and which let in cold air or rain. Finishing the installation of the new Smart Board system the school received so that all the boards would be mounted before the first day of classes. He'd even volunteered to hang the cute puppets she'd found in an antique shop from her classroom ceiling for her. He always went above and beyond. This morning, she really appreciated that.

Emma collected her things off the floor. A stack of artwork she needed to add to the folders students took home every Tuesday and coloring and game sheets she'd copied for this week.

"Ow," she said as something nicked the pad of her middle finger. She lifted the splayed-out pages to find a dagger of glass beneath.

"Are you all right?" Mr. Wilkerson was at her side in an instant. "Let me clean this up," he said. "I'll return everything to your desk, but let me get the glass up before you do anything more."

"I'm fine. I thought I was being careful," she said, sucking the stinging cut into her mouth.

"Let me take care of, uh, of all this for you."

"You're a lifesaver, Mr. Wilkerson. Has anyone told you that today?" She retrieved a bandage from her desk drawer.

"You're the first," he said, smiling shyly.

"Well, I bet I won't be the last. Okay, I'm officially leaving all this to you." Especially since it was going to be even more important to have the art supplies all ready for the kids. Maintaining normalcy would be important today.

For them *and* for her. Because geez.

Soon, the kids started arriving. Emma had been right—they were a great distraction from her less-than-stellar mood. Of course, they immediately noticed the window and asked a million questions, *and* were already bouncing off the wall over the impending winter break. She loved every bit of it.

And those fuzzy pom-poms? They were a huge hit.

Just as they were cleaning up from art, their fuzzy trees, snowmen, and menorahs all laid out to dry, Emma spied Principal Mackey waving to her from outside her door. "Okay, girls and boys. Finish cleaning your areas, wash your hands, and take your seats, please," Emma said before stepping outside her room.

"Miss Kerry," Principal Mackey said, "this is Sheriff Martin. He's filing the report about the vandalism and wanted to speak with you and say hello to your class."

"Hello, Sheriff," Emma said.

Sheriff's hat in hand, the brown-haired man nodded. "Miss Kerry, this shouldn't take long. I walked outside this whole side of the building and there's nothing to indicate who might've done the vandalism. But could you describe to me what you saw and when?"

Emma recounted everything that'd happened after she'd turned on her classroom lights, but honestly, there wasn't much to tell.

The man took a few notes in a small flip pad as she spoke, then tucked it away. "Like I told Principal Mackey, we can have extra patrols ride through school grounds at nights and on the weekends. But it was probably just some kids from the neighborhood. Unfortunately, this kind of thing happens."

"I know," Emma said, her belly giving a weird flip.

He frowned and studied her face. "You sure you're okay, ma'am?"

She nodded and glanced in her window, where the kids' escalating volume indicated that they were getting restless without her. "Yes," Emma said absentmindedly. "I'm just a little on edge because I got mugged on Saturday night and it's left me a little jittery."

"Oh, Emma," Principal Mackey said. "I'm so sorry. What happened?"

She blinked, realizing that she'd just dropped that news out of nowhere. "I was walking home from the store when a man jumped out from behind some bushes and grabbed my purse. Another man saw him and chased him off."

"Did you report this?" Sheriff Martin asked.

Heat infused Emma's cheeks. "No. The mugger was wearing a mask and the man who helped me didn't think the police would be able to do much since I couldn't offer any identifying information."

The sheriff's frown deepened, and his expression made her feel guilty and not a little stupid for not having called the police. "Truth is, he's not entirely wrong. But it's still in your interest to file the report. Get it on record. For when we *do* catch him. And have us step up patrols in the area in the meantime."

"I'm sorry I didn't do it. I was just stunned that it'd happened at all." She glanced into the classroom again. "I'm sorry, Sheriff, do you have everything you need?"

"Yes." He handed her a business card. "If you want to follow up about the mugging, give me a call. I hope you will."

Emma accepted the card, and made a mental note to call him after dismissal. She supposed she'd better at least dot her I's and cross her T's on this. "Thank you. Now, would you like to say hello? I know the kids would love to meet you."

He grinned and nodded. "Absolutely."

She led him in and introduced him, and the kids were immediately enthralled by his uniform, hat, and badge. He kept things light-hearted as he spoke to them about the police working to keep the community safe and inviting them to always feel like they can talk to a police officer, and then he left them with a big stack of crime dog McGruff and Faux Paw techno cat cyber safety stickers.

After that, Emma determined to move on from all the worrisome weirdness of the past few days. Something that was even easier to do when a couple of the other teachers invited her out for a girls' night dinner that evening. With no real family to speak of, the community at Frederick Elementary had become a kind of substitute family for her, and they'd clearly known exactly what she needed.

Thankfully, she didn't need to tell them everything that'd happened in the past few days because she'd told enough people over lunch in the teacher's room that the story had made its way through the whole faculty. But when a family walked through the front door of their favorite Italian place—the man wearing the same denim-and-black-leather jacket that Caine had—Emma couldn't help but wonder what her friends would think of Caine.

Over a big plate of pasta, Emma asked, "What do you all know about that motorcycle club in town?" Her gaze cut to where the family was sitting in the far corner of the restaurant. A dark-haired man, a blond-haired woman, and two boys, probably about first and fifth graders if she were to guess.

"The Raven Riders?" Alison Bard asked in a low voice. Two years older than Emma, she taught one of the other kindergarten sections and had been a mentor and friend since Emma's first day six years before. "They run the race track outside of town. Green Valley. I've been to a few of the races there before."

Catalin Mendoza, their newest kindergarten teacher, nodded. "Me, too. I heard that they provide protective services for people in bad situations. I don't know how that works though. Why?"

Emma twirled her fork in her pasta and recalled Caine talking about working in security. Was that possibly what he'd meant? "The man that tried to stop the mugging belongs to that club."

Her friends' eyes went wide. "Wait," Catalin said. "Are you telling me that you were saved by a *biker* and we're just hearing that detail?"

Smirking, Emma nodded. "It wasn't really pertinent to the story."

Catalin looked like she might swallow her tongue, and glanced at Alison to see if she was as aghast. "Is she serious right now?"

Alison laughed and nodded. "Leave it to you to leave out the best detail, Em. So tell us about your biker."

Her biker. As if. She shrugged. "He was…I don't know…" Emma struggled to think of a description that would do the man any justice.

"She's speechless," Alison said, chuckling.

Catalin's brown eyes were wide as saucers. "She's totally speechless."

Emma couldn't help but laugh. "No, no. It's just that he's unlike anyone I've ever met before. Tall, dark, and intimidating on the outside, but then he had this kinda killer dry humor and was really sweet to me."

Her friends traded a look, and then Catalin said, "When are you going to see him again?"

Shaking her head, Emma swallowed a bite of her noodles. "I didn't get his number."

"Em!" Alison said.

"I could go ask that guy," Cat said in a total deadpan as she thumbed toward where the other Raven sat with his family.

"Don't you dare," Emma said, chuckling—and realizing how much lighter she felt after hanging out with her friends. Even if their teasing was at her expense. And it didn't hurt that she'd followed up with Sheriff Martin after school and filed a report on her mugging. "I can't thank you enough for taking me out tonight. I needed to shake off this funk."

"Always," Alison said. "You know that."

Catalin nodded. "I agree, but I was only half joking about asking that guy."

Emma made a face she *hoped* communicated that she would have to kill her if she made a move toward that Raven.

Shrugging, Catalin grabbed a piece of Italian bread from the basket. "Suit yourself. But if you have a way of tracking down Mr. Tall, Dark, Sweet, and Intimidating, why wouldn't you?"

It was a question still rattling around in her brain as sleep eluded her again that night. And it ensured that, when she did finally nod off, Caine's icy-blue stare starred in all her dreams.

Chapter 5

There was only one thing that really scared Caine, and tonight was the second fucking time in the past five months that the Ravens had been forced to deal with it.

Fire.

That fear was a stupid fucking thing to feel when he'd arrived after the fire department had doused most of the flames. It hadn't happened to him. And he wasn't the one fighting it. Still, standing on the street outside of Ana Garcia's downtown row house, Caine struggled to force away the memories that explained just why he hated fire so goddamn much.

Memories of a trapped little girl. Scorched skin. A two-story fall…

Sonofabitch.

Standing beside him, his brother Phoenix Creed shook his head. "This is fucking bullshit."

Caine nodded, seething that this had happened right under their noses. On the Ravens' watch. Breaking glass had alerted Ana that something was amiss, allowing her to call 9-1-1 and flee the house in plenty of time. And the close proximity of the downtown fire station meant that the responders had been able to get here fast and confine the worst of the damage to the front of the first floor. So Ana would eventually be able to live here again. In the meantime, she'd be safe living in one of the cabins on their compound—where Dare had already taken her about a half hour before, right after she'd finished talking to the sheriff.

So, as crises went, this one had turned out much better than it might've. Not that it made Caine feel one damn bit better.

"Question is, what are we going to do about it?" He arched a brow at Phoenix, whose expression was set in a dark scowl. One that Caine understood, not just because they both felt like they'd dropped the ball here. But also because Phoenix had been the one to bring Ana's case to the Ravens months before, and he felt a certain investment in her situation as a result.

Phoenix's eyes narrowed as he watched the firefighters walk through the burned-out first floor, and the anger he wore made the jagged scar he had from eye to ear look that much fiercer. "If this comes back as arson, like we think? Apparently, I'm going to hell, because I'm gonna take this fucking pastor down."

"I'm a hundred percent sure I already have a reserved parking place down there, so consider me your right-hand man." Caine clapped Phoenix on the shoulder, and the guy gave him a nod.

Though Caine considered the Raven Riders his family and absolutely knew each and every brother would have his back in a heartbeat, he'd never felt especially close to any of them. It wasn't that he didn't put in his time around the club. Hell, he'd served on the board for years now as sergeant-at-arms, so he spent more than a little time with the other board members, including Phoenix and Dare, their leader. But between Caine's belief that he was safer keeping to himself and his gut-deep fucking fear that no one wanted him around—and that no one would like what they found if he ever let them get close, anyway, his walls remained up. Way up. Even with his brothers.

Except, recently, with Phoenix.

Which was maybe because of some shit that'd gone down at Dare's house a few months before—and some things that he and Phoenix had had to make right. Together. And maybe it was also because several other members of the inner circle of the club's board had gone and fallen for the women in their lives, which resulted in Phoenix and Caine spending more solo time hanging out than ever before. And maybe it was because the death of Phoenix's only other living relative had given them yet something else in common—life had left them riding alone, whether they wanted to or not.

So what friendship Caine was capable of feeling, he felt for the guy.

They made for their Harleys, which they'd parked behind the firetrucks down by the intersection. Despite everything else going on, Caine couldn't keep his gaze from stretching across to where he'd first met Emma. Emma Kerry, he'd learned by running an easy public-records search. He looked farther down the street, but couldn't quite make out her house. And it made him fucking itch to go there, check her windows and doors again, maybe even knock on that door and make sure she was still okay.

None of which he was actually going to let himself do. Despite how many times he'd had to resist doing it the past three days.

"What's that look for?" Phoenix asked.

Caine bit back a curse and blanked whatever expression had hit his ugly mug. "No look."

Even pissed off as he was, Phoenix managed a you're-full-of-shit grin. The fucker. "If you say so."

"You going back to the clubhouse?" Caine asked, changing the subject.

"I don't know. I'm fucking wired now. Wanna go to the Pit Stop and get a beer and some chili cheese fries? Or, hell, ride up to Mitzi's?" Phoenix asked.

Neither the old biker bar nor the gentlemen's club located up Maryland's Interstate 70 held any interest for Caine. He wasn't hungry, and he wasn't looking for some cheap hook-up. Hell, he hadn't even checked the message boards since he'd gotten home late on Saturday night. Or, more accurately, early on Sunday morning.

In other words, since he'd left Emma's. And even though he didn't want to examine that too closely, he was examining *the fuck* out of that. Because she kept invading his thoughts. For three days now, she'd been in his head when he worked, when he rode, when he tried to sleep. When he took himself in hand and groaned in the quiet of his room. And it was a fucking problem.

"Not tonight," Caine said, reaching his bike first.

"Dude, you are *not* leaving me hanging."

Straddling the bike, Caine smirked. "You don't need a wingman, Creed. The women love you."

He pulled a face that held none of the anger from moments before. "Well, *yeah*. But that's not the point." *There* was the return of Ravens' favorite playboy smartass.

Caine's Harley came to life on a low growl.

"You suck at wingmanning," he said.

"I suck at reassuring."

"No kidding…"

Jesus. Enough already. "I am shit for people skills. You just figuring this out?"

Phoenix chuckled and held out a hand. *"Fine."* Caine clasped palms with the guy, and Phoenix held on for an extra beat and nailed him with a stare. "'Night, *brother.*"

Caine nodded, appreciating the sentiment. "Now get the fuck out of here." He strapped on his helmet, tugged the black neck-warmer and mouth mask into place, and slid on his gloves.

Laughing, Phoenix made for his Harley. They pulled U-eys together, but parted ways at the intersection—Phoenix turning toward the Pit Stop, and Caine going straight.

Past Emma's.

Without really meaning to, he slowed down. The house was dark except for the lit tree in her living room window, and he wondered if those lights being on meant that she was still awake. Then he asked himself why he cared. And if he was truly stupid enough to believe that some sweet kindergarten teacher would want anything to do with a guy like him.

Right. He revved the bike and took off like a shot down the street.

Because he didn't have an answer for those questions. At least, no answers that he fucking liked.

* * * *

Emma pulled back her bedroom curtain…too late to know if the biker who'd ridden by her house was the one about whom she couldn't stop thinking.

She'd been up since the sirens had woken her over an hour ago, since realizing that a house just down the street had been on fire. She'd lived in this house nearly her whole life and hadn't experienced as much excitement in all that time as she had during the past few days. Not that excitement was the right word. Excitement didn't give you nightmares, and it didn't leave you gasping awake, sure that you'd heard something, and surely it didn't have you deciding you must've imagined it because your dog lay perfectly calm.

Sipping the hot tea she'd made, she sat on the edge of her bed and thought for the hundredth time about what Catalin had said. Why shouldn't she try to get in touch with Caine?

Besides the fact that he was a member of a biker club and that was potentially a little…intimidating.

And besides the fact that he hadn't tried to get in touch with her?

And besides the fact that she might put herself out there only to learn for sure that he'd not given her his number for a reason?

"Yeah, except for all of that," she whispered to the quiet room. Chewy lifted and cocked his little head, making her smile.

She finished the last of her tea and crawled back under the covers.

In the darkness, she saw Caine straddling his bike. Those long legs spread wide. Beat-up boots scuffing the ground. His club cut-off jacket hanging off those broad shoulders, as intriguing as it was menacing. Those strange pale eyes flashing in the dimness. The fullness of his lips the only thing that looked soft on his whole body.

Heat rolled through Emma's blood, pooling sensation low in her belly. Okay, maybe there was *one thing* that qualified as excitement the past few days…because thoughts of Caine had been setting off these reactions within her since the man had been in her house five days before.

Emma squeezed her thighs together, the friction good but not nearly enough. It was too soft, too timid, too…tame. Everything she imagined Caine wouldn't be.

Would his hands grasp her roughly? Would those full lips be hard or soft against her mouth, her throat, her breasts? Was the tattooed body beneath his clothes as lean and masculine as it looked? Would his hips move with fevered urgency or in a slow, teasing grind, and would his words be sweet or dirty against her skin?

Those were the imaginings that had her hand slipping down her body and threading under the waistband of her panties to where she was already wet. Just from thoughts of a man she'd met for only a few hours but who'd somehow invaded her mind.

Her fingers moved in slick, fast circles, and her hips strained upward into her own touch. It took almost no time at all until she was holding her breath and coming, a little cry spilling out of her into the quiet of her room, her body shaking against the bed.

"Jesus, Caine, what did you do to me?" she whispered, pulse racing, heart pounding.

That was the moment she knew she was going to try to find him.

Because if she didn't try, she'd always wonder. Always *regret*. And having lost so many people she cared about during her life, regret was the emotion she most despised. Because Emma had learned first-hand that life was finite, and none of us were replaceable, and death was capricious and sudden.

So, regret? She didn't have time for that.

Emma turned on her side and curled into a ball, and Chewy came closer, relocating himself into a little ball against the crook of her knees. And in the peaceful, satisfied quiet, she knew exactly what to do.

Dutch's.

She'd go talk to the baker woman. Haven. Caine had said she was the club president's fiancée, so she'd have to know him. Right?

The moment the plan cemented in her mind, sleep finally took over, real and deep, for the first time in days.

Chapter 6

Thursday afternoon found Emma walking through the door of Dutch's, a downtown hole-in-the-wall with a long soda fountain with spinning stools and red-and-white booths that had miniature jukeboxes on the walls above each table. And, of course, there was that massive dessert case right as you walked in the door.

At just a few minutes before five, it was a little early for the dinner crowd, so Emma had her pick of seats. She slipped onto one of the stools at the bar and pulled a menu from the rack behind the napkin holder.

"Good evening, young lady," came a man's voice. "What can I get you to drink?"

She looked up into the smiling brown face of an older man whose nametag read "Dutch."

"Hi," she said, returning the smile. The man had a welcoming quality about him that put her at ease. No mean feat given the way her stomach had been doing loop-the-loops in anticipation of asking a stranger about a guy she'd met. "Chocolate milkshake and a water, please."

"Coming right up."

She watched him as he moved from scooping the ice cream to pouring the milk and chocolate sauce in to sliding the metal cup onto an old-time-looking blender. He poured the shake into a glass cup and topped it with a swirl of whipped cream, and then brought both containers over to her.

Emma grinned. "I love when you get the extra in the mixing container."

"Me, too," he said with a wink. "When I opened this place thirty-seven years ago, that was one touch I absolutely knew I'd be doing. Know what you'll be having?"

She ordered a turkey club and then ignored the butterflies in her belly to ask, "Is Haven working tonight?"

The smile he gave her spoke of an affection for the woman. "She's in the back putting the finishing touches on a few cakes. I'll let her know you were asking for her."

"Thank you," she said as he made his way down the counter. She took a long pull on the straw, and the chocolate was cold and rich on her tongue. Oddly, she preferred ice cream in the winter time, even though it meant her hands were probably going to be cold for the rest of the night.

The bell over the front door jingled, and Emma did a double take. Two men wearing Raven Riders jackets came through the door, one with longish dark brown hair and a harsh-looking face, even when he smiled. The other had shorter, wavy brown hair. They slid onto two stools a few down from her and grabbed menus as they talked animatedly about something having to do with cars.

Despite the ice cream in her mouth and the chilled air that had poured in with the bikers, heat filled Emma's face. Because how in the world was she supposed to ask Haven about Caine…with two other members of his club sitting right there?

It took everything she had to not flee. But then a pretty woman with long blond hair pulled back in a ponytail came out through the swinging door carrying a cake platter in each hand, and her gaze landed on Emma. This had to be Haven. Which pretty much meant, *crap*, there was no escape for her now.

No regrets, Em.

Right.

The conversation from the Ravens at the counter fell away as both men focused on the woman. She put down the heavy-looking platters and smiled at them in return.

"Aw, Haven, you shouldn't have," the man with the wavy hair said.

"I'd make you a cake any old day, Jagger Locke. Just name it." She gave his hand an affectionate pat. And then she moved down to the other man. "*Hi.*"

Just that one word communicated so much pleasure that Emma

couldn't look away even though she was fully aware that she was staring. And then the way he looked at her should've come with a warning label. *Caution: Hot.*

"Hi, pretty girl." He pushed up from his seat and leaned his upper body across the counter. His hand cupped the back of her neck as he kissed her. Just one *thorough* kiss.

Wow. *That*...that was the sweetest, hottest thing Emma had seen in a long time. She forced her gaze back to her milkshake and took another long drink.

The woman took their order and entered it into a touch screen, and then she made her way to Emma just as Dutch brought out her oversized sandwich and fries. "Hi, I'm Haven. Dutch said you asked for me."

Emma was one hundred percent aware that both bikers had just looked her way, and she thought it was entirely possible that she might swallow her tongue. So she started with something that was both true and easy. "Hi, I'm Emma. I was raving about the peanut butter cookies to a friend of mine, and he mentioned you're the new baker here. So I wanted you to know how amazing I think they are. I'm, like, never going to try to make peanut butter cookies of my own again."

Haven laughed and gave a little nod. "Why, thank you."

Dutch bumped his shoulder against Haven's. "Hiring this woman was the smartest thing I've done in a long time. See? Even old dogs can learn new tricks."

"You're not old, Dutch. You're distinguished," Haven said, grinning up at the older man whose black hair was shot through with gray. A family came through the door and made for one of the booths.

Laughing, Dutch moved to greet the new arrivals. "Tell that to my hip."

Emma smiled as she ate and watched the banter that shot back and forth between Dutch, the Raven Riders, and Haven. When she was about halfway finished, Emma began debating from which of those cakes she was taking a slice home for later.

Haven came by again. "Can I get you anything else?"

"A box for the rest of my sandwich, please. And can you tell me about those cakes? Despite my milkshake, I think I need some dessert to go."

Haven grinned. "The white one is an eggnog cake, which is basically a rum-soaked butter layer cake with a spiced meringue buttercream."

Emma blinked. "That sounds...amazing."

"The chocolate one is a chocolate peppermint crunch cake. And then there's also a more traditional triple chocolate layer cake and a gingerbread layer cake. What can I tempt you with?"

"How do people even choose?"

"There's only one answer here," the wavy-haired Raven said, pulling Emma's attention back to the bikers. "One of each."

Haven put her hands on her hips. "I mean, I can't disagree."

Chuckling, Emma nodded. "Except then I'd slip into a sugar coma and no one would ever hear from me again. How about the eggnog cake?"

"Good choice," Haven said. She cut and boxed a thick slice, then put both of Emma's boxes into a bag. "By the way, who told you I was the new baker here?"

The question caught her off guard, but only because she'd been trying to think how she might work in asking about Caine—in front of his freaking club members—in a way that sounded totally casual. And here Haven had gone and done it for her. "Oh, uh, Caine?"

Haven frowned. "Caine McKannon?"

Caine McKannon. If that was his name, it was as much rough sex on a stick as he was. A thought that threatened to infuse her face with even more heat.

Emma shook her head. "I don't know his last name. But he's, um, also a Raven Rider." She could feel the men's gazes on her without even looking. But then she did look, and sure enough, they were studying her. The one she now knew was Dare, the club's president, wore an expression like she was a puzzle he couldn't quite solve. Her face felt like it was on fire. "Anyway, yeah."

"Wow, okay," Haven said, giving a little chuckle and exchanging a glance with Dare. "Well, that's him, all right. How did he come to mention that I work here?"

Why did they all seem so...surprised that Caine might've talked to her? "It's kind of a long story." She stirred what was left of her milkshake just to have something to do with her hands. "That started with him chasing off a man who was mugging me and ended with him telling the locksmith I called what kind of additional security my house needed. In the middle, we ate cookies, and I had some of your peanut butters. When I said I got them here, he mentioned knowing you."

They were all still looking at her. Totally confused.

Emma gulped down some water.

Then Haven's expression went soft. "Aw, that's actually…well, that's a Raven for you."

If they hadn't had an audience, Emma would've asked the woman to explain what she meant. But she at least had an inkling, especially after what Catalin had said at dinner the other night. The Ravens offered protective services. Which Caine had absolutely done for her. And it was also clear that Haven thought the world of the men in this club—and that those feelings weren't just for her fiancé, Dare. Emma thought about the affectionate way Haven had interacted with the man she'd called Jagger and how appreciative her tone had been just then about what Caine had done. And it was clear that the woman thought all these men were good, decent guys.

Even though Caine could be intimidating and gruff, it was the same conclusion that Emma had ultimately made about him after they'd spent hours together.

Emma paid her bill and slipped into her coat. And then she finally womaned up to do what it was she'd wanted to do since she first arrived at the restaurant. "So, do you know how I can reach Caine? I didn't get his number, and I wanted to thank him for everything he did for me." She didn't direct her question to Haven alone, because clearly all three of these people knew Caine.

Dare shifted on his stool, the others clearly deferring to him. "He's kind of a private person. But if you'd like me to pass on your number, I can do that."

Kind of a private person… Yeah, Emma could see that. "Oh, of course." She approached the man and rattled off her cell phone number when he gave her the signal.

Dark, serious eyes searched her face, then Dare nodded. "Got it. And I'm glad Caine was able to help you."

"Me, too." For a second, she was unsure how to extricate herself, and then she finally nodded and made a move for the door. "Merry Christmas," she managed. Out on the sidewalk, she felt like she could breathe again. What was it about the members of the Raven Riders that made them so freaking intense to talk to?

She'd only made it a few buildings down when a man's voice called her name.

"Emma?"

She turned to find Dare leaning out the door of Dutch's. "Yes?"

"Are you walking? Do you need a ride somewhere?" he asked.

It took her brain a second to compute what he'd just offered her, and then a flood of warmth spilled through her chest. The same kind of warmth that Caine arranging to get her medicine had unleashed that night they'd met. Who *were* these guys?

"No, I drove." She pointed down the block. "I'm just a few doors further down. But thank you for asking."

A single nod. "Be safe." He ducked back inside.

Emma stood there kinda stunned. And in the wake of Dare's kindness, her desire to see Caine again was even stronger than before she'd arrived.

That made her belly fall, though, because everything was in his court. Dropping by her house. Calling. Everything.

All she could do was wait.

* * * *

Three pairs of eyes swung Caine's way as he stepped inside Dutch's. Dare and Jagger sat at the bar, ogling him like he had three heads. And Haven's whole face lit up.

"What?" he asked, wary as he made for the open stool next to Jagger.

Haven grinned excitedly at him, which was fucking weird. No one reacted to him entering a room that way. "What can I get you, Caine?"

"Black coffee. Thanks." He peered to his left, where his brothers were still all about the three heads. "What the hell is up with you two?"

"We met someone you know," Dare said matter-of-factly.

Haven brought his coffee, and he took a long sip, then shrugged. "Okay?"

"A very cute blond someone," Jagger said, trying to school his expression. Trying and fucking failing.

Caine gave a bored sigh. And even though he knew exactly who they were talking about—hell, he could almost *feel* the echo of her energy in here now—he played it cool. "That doesn't narrow it down very fucking much, now, does it."

Jagger smirked.

"You want something to eat?" Haven asked, eyeballing him like she knew he was playing dumb.

Which of course he was. "You got chicken noodle tonight?"

She nodded. "That's all?"

"Yeah," he said. Not that he usually had much of an appetite, but his asshole friends ambushing him with their knowledge of Emma had chased away his ache for food.

His phone buzzed in his pocket, and he fished it out and unlocked the home screen. The text was from Dare. He frowned at the guy sitting four feet from him and then opened the message.

Emma's number is 301-555-1851. She asked to get in touch with you.

His gut squeezed, and the question was out of his mouth before he'd meant to say it. "Is she okay?"

"Ohhh. Which *she* would that be again?" Jagger asked, his expression full of mirth. Even though that was irritating as shit, Caine couldn't hold it against the guy. For months now, Jagger had been uncharacteristically serious—his old easy-going manner dimmed somehow, ever since he'd been released from jail back in November. He'd served almost four months for a crime he hadn't committed. And even though he'd been exonerated, the experience had marked him in a way that they all saw.

So, fine, Caine wasn't going to flip his shit. This time. "Yeah, yeah. D?"

Dare nodded. "She's fine. Just feeling grateful." He arched a dark brow that communicated everything Caine needed to know—namely that she'd told them what he'd done. And not done. "Anyway, sounds like you did good."

Caine's gaze cut to Dare's harsh face. "The fucker got away. Nothing good about that."

Haven delivered his soup and a big stack of salty crackers, just like she knew he liked. And that little personal touch... It wasn't something he was used to receiving, because there weren't many people who had any reason to know his likes and dislikes that well. "It sounds like you stood up for her, Caine," she said in a quiet voice, "and that all by itself can mean a lot to a person if it's not something anyone's done for them before."

Her words hit him in places he didn't like to think too much about. *"You always look out for me..."*

Caine swallowed hard against the memory of Grace's voice. And Haven helped pull him back to the present when she placed a square white pastry box on the counter next to him.

"What's that?" he managed.

"A little something for Emma. It sounds like she's a fan of my peanut butter cookies. I baked these fresh, and I was thinking you could deliver some to her. You know, for me."

Caine blinked. Then his gaze narrowed. First on the box, then on his brothers, who were watching him like he might be a bomb about to detonate, and then, finally, on the petite woman standing in front of him. Her expression as innocent as a fucking newborn babe.

He was being played here.

He knew he was.

But he wasn't giving them the satisfaction of a reaction. So he shrugged one shoulder and dug back into his soup. "I'll see what I can do."

Which translated in McKannonese to *when hell freezes over.* The others just didn't realize it.

"Okay," Haven said, excitement plain in her tone.

So fucking played.

He gulped the soup down, pocketed the crackers, and paid his bill. Then, just barely swallowing back a groan, he took the fucking box of cookies, too.

Not once did he let himself examine why their little ploy made him feel like a layer of his skin had been flayed off, exposing all his nerves to the slightest excruciating touch. And no way was he actually going to Emma's. Instead, he went home. Worked on his bike for a few hours, blaring rock music drowning out the voices in his head. Then he fell into the couch with the TV playing, knowing there was every likelihood he'd end up sleeping right there—for however long his brain would actually allow him to shut down.

Which turned out not to be very long. Because that cookie box was sitting on his coffee table. Taunting him. Tormenting him. Tempting him.

Problem was? Caine wasn't a very strong man. And the things someone good and wholesome and, just, *normal* like Emma Kerry might tempt him with were the kinds of things that would break him if he ever let himself imagine—for even one second—he could actually have them.

Caine knew that in his gut, in his long dead heart, and in his memories. Jesus, he could *hear* the sound of the breaking even now. The sick wet crunch of it.

So he turned over and faced the back of the couch. And ignored that box like a motherfucker. It was safer that way.

Chapter 7

Caine spent nearly all day on Friday helping Jagger handle a maintenance issue at the club's racetrack. Green Valley brought in the biggest part of the Raven Riders' revenue—through avenues both legal and less so—and they all pitched in to help Jagger, their Race Captain—whenever he asked.

Today, Caine had appreciated the distraction.

From the fact that he'd slept like shit. And from the fact that he knew exactly what had kept him staring up at the dark ceiling all night.

Those damn cookies. Or, more specifically, the thought of taking those damn cookies to a certain pretty blonde.

Riding home after a long day's work out in the cold, Caine forced his thoughts to focus on more immediate concerns. A hot shower. Maybe some food, because the saltines he'd eaten for lunch weren't really cutting it. Yeah, he'd have one of his protein shakes, at least.

Suddenly his phone started blowing up, judging by the constant vibrations in his pocket.

As soon as he parked in the gravel drive in front of his trailer, he checked his cell.

His gut started a slow fall. He should've known he'd only be able to outrun this situation for so long. Though, when Jagger hadn't teased him at all about it, a part of him thought he might've skirted the issue for today. No such luck.

Haven wants to know if Emma enjoyed the cookies, Dare had written about eight minutes before. Making it clear there would be no skirting.

A minute later: *Did you take them?*

Two minutes after that: *Tell me you took them.*

And one more, from just a minute ago: *Dude.*

Caine dismounted his bike and made his way inside, his fingers moving as he typed and deleted and typed again. Finally, he replied, *Not yet.*

Dare's response was immediate. *When? I know you're not thinking about wasting those fucking cookies, right?*

Those. Fucking. Cookies.

Caine didn't have to ask why Dare was making a federal case out of them. First, because Haven made them, and the sun rose and set in her eyes for Dare. Second, because Haven had specifically asked Caine to do something for her, and no way was Dare going to allow that favor to go undone—even if it'd been a total set-up.

Right Caine? popped up on his cell.

"Aw, sonofabitch," Caine bit out under his breath as he let himself into his place.

On a sigh, he resolved to do what he had to do. *Tonight*, he replied. He'd take the fucking cookies and be done with the whole thing. Once and for all.

Good man, Dare messaged.

Caine rolled his eyes. *Fuck you*, he messaged back.

LOL asshole was Dare's only reply.

He made straight for his bedroom and shed his clothes and the Under Armour base layers that were a necessity for winter bike-riding onto the low futon bed. It was the only piece of furniture in the room, not counting the row of milk crates that held what clothing he owned. Extreme poverty as a child had made him a saver and a minimalist as an adult. For years now, he rarely spent money on anything unless he absolutely needed it. Not to mention that he was half convinced that, somehow, the bottom would fall out of his life again just like it had when he was a kid. And when that happened, at least the money he'd socked away from what the club paid him to run security for its protective services, not to mention his cut of the Ravens' off-the-books activities, would be there to catch him.

In the bathroom, he set the shower to scalding and got in while it was still warming up. He made quick work of washing his hair, which was short but still much longer than usual. Normally, he kept it shaved close to better mask the fact that a section at the base of his skull no longer grew right, but he'd slacked off the past month or so and hadn't gotten around to doing it.

When he was done with his hair, he took longer washing his body. He stretched to reach the rough, twisted skin of his back and right shoulder. He scoured his hands, his fingernails, his feet, his armpits, his dick. And then he did it all again. Harder. Caine wanted the grease gone from working on his bike the night before. He wanted the sweat gone from helping out at the track all day. He wanted every bit of the sheer fucking worthlessness gone that had built up around him from a lifetime of cruel words and despicable acts.

If he was going to show up at Emma Kerry's house, he wanted all of it gone.

That feeling was almost certainly why, once he was dried off and dressed again, he didn't bother trying to eat, not even a shake. As a kid, he'd done everything he could to avoid giving the monsters who'd run his foster home the satisfaction of seeing him cry or beg or yearn. Including for food. By the age of twelve, he'd already worn hunger like a badge of honor. Now, his system handled stress by shutting down any appetite he might've still possessed. Shutting it down hard. Which was one of the reasons he didn't often join his brothers in meals at the clubhouse. That was better than being asked questions about why he wasn't eating.

By the time he was knocking on Emma's door, he was all kinds of on edge. Which was just fucking perfect.

The heavy *click* of the new deadbolt sounded. The door swung open. And then there she was.

Blue eyes going wide, a slow smile brightening her face, and so fucking pretty in a soft pink sweater and a pair of form-fitting jeans that showed off the sweet, feminine curves of her hips. Sitting in the crook of Emma's arm, Chewy's furry tail wagged in a steady beat. "Caine." Her voice was full of pleasant surprise. "Hi. Uh, come in."

Why did he suddenly feel like a teenager? Bumbling through talking to a girl for the first time. "Oh, uh, no. I just—"

Beeping rang out from somewhere inside. "Come in, come in. Sorry, that's the timer on the oven." She turned away from the door and made for the kitchen.

For a moment Caine stared at the empty spot where she'd just stood, and then he heaved a breath and stepped inside. Where it smelled *amazing*. Like garlic and baked cheese. His stomach squeezed, hunger rearing its ugly head.

Little noises reached him from the kitchen—a dish against the counter, the oven door closing, Emma talking to the dog as its nails clicked on the floor. But Caine hung in the living room, close to the door. While he waited, his gaze landed on the Christmas tree and a photo ornament shaped like a snowflake. He leaned in. It was a much-younger Emma with an older woman. The family resemblance was plain to see.

"Hey, sorry," Emma said, rushing back into the room.

Caine reared back from the tree and found Emma watching him. He held out the box. "For you," he blurted.

A little smile grew on her face. "What's this?"

"A gift. From Haven," he rushed to add. "'Cause you said you liked them."

Emma lifted the lid. Her grin was like the sun shining after a storm. Bright and restoring. "I can't believe she did this. But I'm really glad she did. And you, too."

"I was just the delivery guy." He stuffed his hands in his jeans pocket. "And now that I've delivered them—"

"Stay for dinner."

Caine blinked. "What?"

Her cheeks turned the same soft pink as her sweater. It was stunning. Not just because she was so pretty...

Asking him to dinner had made her blush. For a long moment, all he could do was stare. He considered himself better than average at reading people, and that little uncontrollable, physical display of emotion seemed to reveal that she felt like she was laying herself bare.

Over him.

The realization hit him right in the chest, and he had absolutely no idea what to make of it. He was used to people coming at him with wariness or revulsion. And he'd finally come to trust the loyalty his brothers gave him. Hell, even naked animal desire came his way from time to time.

But this sweet vulnerability? Her apparent belief that someone like him wouldn't want someone like her? That was new territory for him. In every regard.

How could he not want the sweetness she was offering? But how could he open himself up to wanting it?

She licked her lips and met his gaze head on, letting him see her sincerity in a way he found so damn brave. "We never got to have that sandwich the other night. And I made a whole pan of lasagna. Stay."

* * * *

He wasn't going to stay. Emma could see it in those pale eyes, in the way his lean body was already angled toward her foyer, in how rigidly he held himself.

The longer he went without answering, the more an awkward tension filled the space between them. Until Emma was nearly dying of embarrassment and wishing the floor would swallow her up. She'd been so excited that he'd come back that she'd made all kinds of assumptions that apparently weren't true. And as she thought back over the minutes since he'd arrived, she realized he'd only come in because she'd needed to get the lasagna out of the oven before the top got too brown.

And then she'd put him on the spot. A spot he clearly didn't know how to get out of.

She shook her head. "Never mind. It's okay—"

"No," he said, his brow cranking down over that rugged face. "I'll...I'll stay."

Emma studied the white box in her hands, her belly doing a weird twisty thing. She didn't want him to stay because he felt cornered into it, so she gave him the out. "You don't have to, Caine. I didn't mean to make you uncomfortable. But thank you for delivering the cookies."

"Fuck," he bit out under his breath.

Her gaze snapped to meet his, which roiled with emotion she couldn't name and didn't understand. The connection made her pulse race and her skin heat. Or maybe that was because the man was so freaking sexy. His intensity. His harsh face paired with those strange eyes and full lips. His raw masculinity with all its hard angles and rough edges.

"It's just... I'm not very..." He shook his head, and Emma could've groaned for want of knowing what he was trying to say. "I want to stay. If it's still okay."

A tendril of hopefulness curled into her chest. "Of course it's okay. I wouldn't have invited you if I didn't want you. To stay, I mean. For dinner." *Oh my God, stop talking, Em!*

He nodded, a hint of what she thought might be humor playing around his mouth. "Dinner sounds good." He pushed the black knit cap off his head, and then smoothed his hand over the sexy mess the hat had made of his short hair.

"Good. Great." She smiled and took a deep breath. Clearly a week of fantasizing about this man had fried her brain, if the spectacular stream of gibberish falling out of her mouth was any indication. "Then let's eat."

Emma led him into the kitchen and wondered why she was so much more nervous around him tonight. Part of it was because the dynamic between them had changed. That first night, he'd been her protector and given her a sense of safety. Now, he'd become her secret tormentor and made her feel entirely vulnerable. It made no matter that he hadn't intended those things. It didn't make them any less true.

He'd saved her. He'd intrigued her. He'd left her wanting more.

"Smells fucking amazing," he said as they stepped into her kitchen. The compliment relaxed her and made her grin, but before she could respond, he blurted, "Shit, sorry for the language. Force of habit."

She smirked. "I'm a teacher, Caine. Not a nun. My ears aren't sensitive." She gathered plates, silverware, and napkins. It was maybe silly how much pleasure she got out of preparing to set a table for two, but since her grandmother had died, she hadn't entertained here much. Instead, friends tended to invite her to hang out with them. Just like Alison had for Christmas dinner. "Someone willing to risk themselves to protect another person, rather than just being a bystander, can say whatever they want as far as I'm concerned."

"You're a kindergarten teacher," he said, his eyes tracking her every movement.

Hands full, she moved toward the table and then laid out the place settings. "And?" she said with a little laugh. "What does that mean?"

His gaze narrowed. "Kindergarten teachers are like...paragons of innocence and sweetness."

Emma waited for the punch line, humor bubbling up inside her. And then she started chuckling. "Oh, man, would my friend Catalin get a kick out of that." She shook her head, laughter still bubbling up inside her. "When she gets worked up over something, she swears like a sailor. That's just a reputation because our job entails being cheerful and patient, and having a willingness to not take yourself too seriously, and playing with glitter and fuzzy pom-poms alongside teaching letters and numbers and social skills. Grab us some orange soda?"

He nodded, then waved a hand at what covered her fridge door. "This is what I mean. You influence the minds of the littlest kids and they adore you for it. Look." He bent down to read one of the pictures. "Case in point. This one says 'Miss Kerry, best teacher ever'."

Actually, it said *best teesher ever*, which was even cuter. "But none of that means I'm Mary Freaking Poppins," she said, amused, even as she wondered why it was important to him that she might be innocent and sweet. Which, given how many times she'd masturbated to imagining being with him, she didn't really think she was... He turned with two bottles in hand, his expression entirely confused. "Mary Poppins. The magical, always cheery and perfect British nanny?"

"That's not really...my speed," he managed.

"Well, you get the point." Grinning, Emma brought the Italian bread to the table, then scooped big squares of lasagna onto their plates. "I'm just a normal girl trying to feed a boy some homemade lasagna."

Plates in hand, she turned—and nearly walked right into Caine.

"Oh, geez, sorry. I almost dumped this all over you. See? Definitely not perfect."

He stepped to her right to let her past, but she went to that side, too. Then they repeated the little dance on the left. She chuckled. He smirked. And then, suddenly, that smirk smoldered and flashed hot. His gaze dropped to her mouth and lingered there a while.

Time slowed as her heart tripped into a sprint. A shiver raced down her spine. Her nipples hardened. It was entirely possible that she was misreading what her body seemed to be feeling, except his eyes were now blazing. She licked her lips, hungry for just...one...taste...

All at once, he shook his head, his brow furrowing. He took one of the plates from her hand. "I got it."

"Sure. Thanks," she managed, wondering if he heard the breathy desire in her voice. Because for a moment there she'd been sure he was going to kiss her. And, damnit, she was disappointed he hadn't.

They settled at her little kitchen table, and Chewy danced around for a moment until Emma signaled for him to lay down. On a resigned grunt, he curled into a ball under the table near her feet.

Emma was just about to dig into the mound of sauce and cheese and noodles on her plate when his words stopped her short.

"I'm not a normal boy, though." Focusing on his plate, he sliced the fork into his food and took a big bite.

"What?"

That icy gaze latched onto hers. "You said you were a normal girl. I'm not... That's not me. Normal. I'm not the guy you invite to dinner. Or take home to meet family."

His words rattled around in her thoughts while she dug into her food, and they ate in silence for a long moment. Why didn't he think he was normal or worthy of being invited in and acknowledged? A little ache set off in her chest, just left of center, because she'd had students who expressed similar sentiments, and a troubled home life was, without exception, behind whatever had given them such negative thoughts about themselves.

Making that connection, she finally began to understand what all his comments tonight were adding up to—an argument about why they wouldn't and couldn't work. Which both tied her belly up in knots, because he didn't think they could work, but also unleashed a strange sensation of tingling lightness in her chest, because he was thinking about the idea of a *them* at all. "Well, I don't have any family for you to meet, so you're safe there."

He swallowed another bite of lasagna and nailed her with a stare. "How do you mean?"

She gave a little shrug. "Never knew my father. My mother died when I was nine. And my grandmother who raised me died three years ago. It's just me. Well, me and Chewy." It made her a little sad to lay it out that way, but she wasn't sad or unhappy. She was generally satisfied with her life. She had a good job she loved. Friends who cared about her. An awesome dog. Plenty of the things she needed.

Caine's brow cranked down. Not like he was displeased, but almost like he was confused. He took another big bite, which was when Emma realized that he'd nearly finished his piece of lasagna while she hadn't eaten quite half of hers.

"How about you?" she asked, wondering what was going on in that mind of his. Caine was definitely *not* someone she'd ever describe as talkative, but she got the impression that there was a thoughtful, complicated mind behind the scowls and silences.

"Ravens are my only family."

Maybe it was the tension suddenly in his shoulders or the way he'd slowed down from eating, but he strongly radiated that this topic wasn't open for discussion. Which no doubt meant there was plenty to discuss, and that it wasn't particularly good. "I met Dare and Jagger."

"I heard," he said.

She chuckled, even though she wasn't sure his tone was approving. "And Haven, too. They seemed nice."

He smirked. "Nice, huh?"

"Are they not nice?" She arched an eyebrow, happy to pull the conversation from whatever had made him so serious to banter around something lighter.

He chuffed out a little laugh. "Haven is nice. Obviously. Jagger…" Caine nodded. "He's one of the best of all of us. And Dare, he's a total hard ass, but when the chips are down, I'd absolutely want him at my side." He cleaned his plate, even going so far as to scoop every little drop of sauce off.

She held out her hand. "Let me get you seconds."

His gaze lifted to hers, and then he shook his head. "It's okay."

"I enjoy seeing you enjoy what I made," she said. She hadn't intended there to be innuendo in what she said, but she heard it nonetheless. And so, it seemed, did he.

He tilted his head and licked his lips, and it made her belly go on a loop-the-loop. Emma was endlessly fascinated with this man's mouth. The softness of those full lips. The way they could press into a harsh line that communicated so much. The words that fell from it—sometimes too blunt, sometimes mysterious, sometimes sarcastic and even a little funny. And then, sometimes, so sweet it stole her breath. She wouldn't mind becoming a lot more acquainted with his mouth. There was no doubt about it.

"Maybe I could have a little more," he said. His voice was low, rough.

She took his plate and rose, and she felt the weight of his gaze on her almost like it was a physical caress. At the stove, she cut a piece as big as the first. As fast as he'd demolished his first helping, it was clear he was hungry. And she remembered how loud his stomach had growled that first night before they'd been interrupted. She was only too happy to feed him.

Ten minutes later, satisfaction rolled through her when he'd cleaned his plate for the second time. "Dessert?" she asked with a grin.

He rubbed a hand over his stomach. "I shouldn't."

"That's not a no. Before you decide, maybe you should know that I don't just have cookies." Grinning, she went to the freezer and pulled out two boxes, then turned and held them up for him. "I also have the mac daddy of ice cream treats—classic Nutty Buddy Sundae Cones and Chocolate Overload Nutty Buddy Super Scoops Sundae Cones."

"The mac daddy, huh?" It was the closest thing she'd ever seen to a full, real smile on Caine's face, and it made him freaking *gorgeous*. His eyes crinkled, and he had the hint of a dimple just on one side.

Emma was entirely sure her jaw was sitting on the kitchen floor. She struggled to pick it up. "Yup," she managed, and then she shook the boxes. "Come on, you know you wanna."

His gaze went from the first box, to the second, then to her. He gave her a slow, blatant, lingering onceover that made her want to tear off her sweater for the heat that flashed through her blood. "You might be right, Emma. I do wanna."

Her heart tripped into a sprint. Because she was pretty sure that she was game for whatever he might want. And why not? She was twenty-seven and single. She didn't need anyone's permission, nor did she require some sort of commitment to consider enjoying a man's company. And more than all of that, no man had ever taunted and tempted and intrigued her the way this one did. Maybe it was that he'd protected her. Maybe it was all the layers she sensed beneath the hard-as-hell exterior. Or maybe it was that killer intensity that ricocheted off of him, some potent elixir of raw masculinity with a dash of danger.

Swallowing hard, she managed a nod. "So, I'll ask again. Dessert?"

Chapter 8

Caine ached into his very bones. Ached with desire and need and lust.

As if Emma Kerry wasn't fucking beautiful and funny and smart. As if she wasn't direct and honest and sincere. As if she hadn't sated his hunger for the first time in...ever. Hell, he couldn't remember the last time he'd allowed himself to eat until he was full. Now she was waving a red flag at him, and he wasn't sure she realized that he was a bull that wanted nothing more than to charge until he'd pinned her to the ground beneath him.

He felt torn in two. Between restraint and letting himself loose. Between doing what was right for both of them and doing what they obviously both wanted. Between being dumbfounded that someone like Emma would want him, and not wanting to question it before she came to her senses and realized she was way too fucking good to be messing around with someone like him. Someone so broken. Someone so unworthy. Someone whose hands were so dirty with the grime of life's underbelly.

"Regular or overload?" she asked again, looking at him like she was throwing down a challenge.

It was the rasp in her tone that did it. That little tell that her physical desire was true, visceral, real snapped the last of his restraint.

Slowly, he rose. Stalked across the kitchen. Took the ice cream from her hands. He reached over and dropped the boxes on the counter, and then he was right back to her again. All up in her space and walking her back until she was trapped. Trapped by him.

"You, Emma. I choose you for dessert." His mouth came down on hers, demanding and firm. And that first brush of skin on skin lit him all the way up. He was rock hard and wound tight, full of need and wonder. What was left of his brain function raged against the recklessness of allowing himself even a single taste of her sweetness. He shouldn't do this. He knew he shouldn't. But he *wanted* to so fucking bad.

Just one good long taste.

On a moan, her lips parted and her arms went around his neck. Caine's tongue sank deep, plundering her mouth like the invader he was. She tasted like orange soda and everything good in the world, and he licked and sucked at every little moan and mewl and gasp she gave him.

He needed to claim every single one. And he wanted more.

Plowing his hands into her silky, soft hair, he boxed her in tighter against the counter, the shifting press of her belly a too-soft tease against his hard dick. But this wasn't going to be about that. He was going to make this about her. About giving her pleasure, not taking his own. If he gave and didn't take, maybe she'd regret it less when she realized what she'd done—and who she'd done it with. And maybe, just maybe, he'd find it easier to walk away when this was over and she came to her senses. Like he knew she would.

"Caine," she rasped around the edge of the kiss.

Fisting his hand in her blond waves, he urged her to tilt her head back. He trailed kisses and licks and nips across her cheek to her ear, her jaw bone, that soft spot on her neck. Downward, to where the slope of her skin met the neck of her sweater. God she was soft and sweet, the little sounds spilling out of her like rays of sunlight in the darkness. So warm and unexpected.

And then he was back at her mouth again like the greedy motherfucker he was. Tasting and exploring and penetrating until she was panting and pushing herself against his cock and he feared he might not be strong enough to keep his dick in his pants where it needed to stay.

Reaching between the tight press of their bodies, he popped the button on her jeans.

Her eyelids lifted slowly, like she was as lust drunk as he was. And he looked her eye to eye as he laid out his intentions. "I need to taste more of you. *All* of you."

"Oh, my God," she whispered, the words puffing against his lips because they were so close. "Taste me."

Caine didn't have to be told twice. He went down to his knees, his hands already working at the denim clinging to her hips. She wore white satin beneath the jeans—of course that was what she wore. And it shouldn't have turned him on even more, but he couldn't deny that it fucking did.

When he had the denim around her knees, he smoothed his calloused hands up the outside of her thighs to her hips, then back down again. He peered up at her, leaned in, and grabbed the edge of the panties with his teeth.

Holding her gaze, he worked them down, too. And then she was bared to him. Bared and fucking beautiful.

He didn't ask a second time, but she nodded anyway. That pretty face so flush, her mouth open and her lips red from their kisses. From *his* kisses.

His gaze fell to the triangle of dark blond at the top of her thighs, and Caine was suddenly ravenous all over again. He worked a hand between her closed thighs and then pushed it up until he'd opened her stance a little and held her ass in his hand. And then he put his mouth on her.

Right. Fucking. There.

His tongue immediately found her wetness and swirled it around until the volume of her moans told him he'd found her clit. And then he was absolutely *relentless*. Licking. Sucking. Flicking. Nipping. Lapping at her until his mouth and chin were wet with her juices and she was thrusting and straining her hips.

"Oh, God, Caine. Oh, God," she rasped. And his name on her lips in this moment was like a prize for a man who'd never before won a contest. He just hoped it didn't raise his hopes that he might win again. Because the odds were always stacked in favor of the house, not the player.

He went at her harder, faster, savoring every gasp, every drop of her arousal, every moment that he could see her like this. Raw and frenzied and hungry. For him. Her hands fell to his head, holding and guiding him, her fingers clenching in a bid to gain purchase in his short hair.

Christ, he could come from this alone. From getting to be the one on his knees making her pussy clench and weep against his mouth.

His thumb slipped into the wetness he was drawing out with his tongue, then teased her pussy and dipped inside her. His grip tightened against her ass, and his fingers slid between her cheeks, two of his fingertips brushing against her rear hole.

The groan she unleashed sounded like the most shattered satisfaction. "Coming, coming," she cried, her pleasure coating his tongue and thumb. Maddeningly curious, Caine pressed his fingertips harder against that hole again, and she nearly buckled over him, her hips shuddering, her orgasm stretching out, her short nails scratching against his scalp. Fuck.

Fuck. The pleasure she got out of him touching her ass while he ate her pussy would be tattooed on his memory for the rest of his life. Which was so damn much better than most of the other things etched there.

"Jesus, Caine," she rasped, still trembling.

He pushed her upright again, one big hand braced against her belly. Because there was no fucking way he wasn't licking her clean. He did, and she let him, even though she must've been terribly fucking sensitive judging by the near pained cries and little pleading begs that spilled out of her mouth.

"Oh, God, please. Please, Caine. I can't... I can't take it... It's so good but it...it's too much."

When he was satisfied, he peered up her body. Their gazes collided, and he snaked his tongue between those soft lips one more time.

Just one last taste.

And then he sucked his thumb clean for good measure, making sure she saw him do it. He wasn't going to hide his enjoyment of her, nor the fact that he could find pleasure in things that crossed lines for some other people. Truth be told, he wasn't sure he had a line at all.

Finally, Caine pulled up those little white panties and put them back into place. Repeated that process with her jeans. Grabbed his hat and got to his feet, his boots a little clumsy and heavy against the floor after being on his knees for so long.

Chewy growled and barked, and then he was suddenly jumping at the door to the back porch.

Emma's head dropped against Caine's chest. "I'm sorry that my dog is cockblocking you," she said, humor plain in her tone. "This is his needs-to-go-out dance."

Well, that made things a little easier for Caine, then, didn't it? "Don't worry about it."

Her hand cupped his dick through his jeans, and Caine was still so aroused that he groaned. Emma bit down on her bottom lip as she stared at his face, and the look she was giving him was so damn sexy. She whispered. "Oh, I'm not worried. I'm just wanting my turn."

Caine nearly shuddered from the erotic promise, and from the fact that he needed to resist it.

Luckily for him, Chewy was going in circles now, barking like it was the new cool thing to do. "Hold that thought," Emma said, smiling at him so damn pretty. Her cheeks were still pink from the exertion of her orgasm. Her hair was still mussed from his hands. Her eyes were still heavy with desire. She made for the door and shook her head as she bent down to give the dog a pat. "What is your problem anyway? Barking like a crazy man. Come on."

Cold air poured in as she flipped on the back porch light and stepped outside. The chill lured Caine out with her, because he was in need of some serious assistance in cooling himself off before he took this thing with her places his gut told him he didn't want it to go.

Chewy went out like a shot, sniffing all over the porch before finally running down the steps and repeating the sniffing circle in the small grassy yard. Flurries spun in the air around them, and Caine wanted to crack his head against the brick wall of her house for noticing how pretty they looked in Emma's golden hair.

"Would you go already, silly dog? You barked to come out and now all you wanna do is sniff," Emma said, peering over the railing.

Chewy finally found a spot to cop a squat, but then he was back to sniffing. Liking the cold, Caine pocketed his hat and inhaled a deep, calming breath, readying himself to walk away when they went back inside.

"No, Chewy!" Emma suddenly called out.

Caine looked into the dimness of the yard in time to see Chewy's tail disappearing through the wooden gate.

"How did that get open?" Emma said, taking off down the steps. "Caine, grab the green bag of treats off the shelf inside the door for me."

Frowning, he did as she asked, and then he jogged them out to where she stood in the alley in a stand-off with Chewy. About fifteen feet away, he looked like he would bolt if she took a step toward him. Caine opened the bag. "Here."

"Thanks," she said, reaching in before crouching with a weird toothbrush-shaped green thing. "Chewy want a Greenie? I know you do." Chewy trotted over like all was right in his world, and Emma scooped him up as he grabbed the treat in his teeth. "I never let him off leash, and on those rare occasions when he escapes, it's not always easy to get him to come back. But Greenies are his favorite, so they're my secret weapon."

Back inside her little yard, she secured the black iron latch on her shoulder-high gate, and Caine frowned. It didn't have an interior lock, but it was otherwise plenty stable. Definitely not the kind of latching system that slipped open by itself. So if Emma hadn't opened it, who had?

Shaking his head, he followed her up onto the porch, and then he froze while she made for the door. Because the storm window on her kitchen window was part-way up.

"What?" she asked, turning to see why he'd stopped.

Caine walked to the window. When he'd done the security check for her last weekend, he'd lifted this window to see how easy it was to open from the outside. He'd been able to work it up about five inches, but no more because something in the old frame was bent, keeping it from going all the way up. That was good – because if Caine couldn't easily lift the lower half of the storm window, an intruder couldn't either.

Except, Caine was ninety-five percent sure that he'd lowered it again. Hadn't he?

"Sorry," he said. "I didn't realize I'd left this up last weekend." He worked it down again, unleashing a metallic screech as the bent frame protested the movement.

"Oh, geez. Don't give it a second thought," Emma said. "Not after everything you did."

Right. Like examining this window. And putting it back in place when he was done. Which he would've sworn he'd done. Lifting his gaze, he looked through the window to Emma's bright kitchen. The position of this window meant that he had a direct view of the L-shaped counter.

The counter against which Caine had just had Emma.

As casually as he could, he peered down at the ground outside the window. The snow hadn't fallen enough to be useful for revealing tracks, but Caine's instincts were screaming at him.

Dog flipping out. Gate being open. Window being up.

Made an equation that Caine really didn't fucking like.

Even though there was no proof that those things actually made any equation at all.

"Something wrong?" Emma asked.

Yes. He shook his head. "Just irritated at myself. Security aside, that did nothing good for your heating bills."

"Seriously, don't worry about it. Come on. Let's go back in." She dropped Chewy on the floor and he took off for the living room. Caine watched as the dog made a circuit around the space before finally retreating to his dog bed, treat still in his teeth.

Yeah, I know something's not quite right too, buddy.

He turned to find Emma clearing the table, so he pitched in carrying dirties to the sink. "Sorry about these," he said, picking up the now room temperature boxes of ice cream.

Emma laughed as she pushed up her sleeves and turned on the faucet. "I would sacrifice Nutty Buddies for a shot at your mouth *any day.*"

He gaped at her, fucking stunned that she'd been that blunt. Jesus. The words wrapped around his cock as if they'd been her fist.

She laughed harder. "I told you I wasn't any nun. Besides, there are more Nutty Buddies where those came from." She rinsed a dish and placed it into the dishwasher.

His gut clenched. "Don't walk up to that store alone again." He hadn't meant for the words to come out that harshly, but following what he'd maybe just stumbled across on her back porch, the thought of her walking around at night again, of getting hurt this time, made him want to break things with his bare hands.

She put another dish into the rack, then looked up at him. "Okay."

He gave a single nod. "I'm...I'm gonna go."

Her expression was almost cartoonish in its surprise. Not that he thought it was funny. He knew he was being abrupt and awkward, but there was no way around it. At some point, it was going to be both of those things. So there was no point putting it off. "Why?"

"Dinner was fantastic," he said, meaning it. The food in his belly made him feel like he had more gas in his tank than he'd had for a very long time. "And...making you come was something I'll never forget. But we should leave it at that."

In a quick glance, her gaze dropped to his crotch.

"*Emma*." Not only was his dick not the problem, but she had no idea that there was a three-way war raging inside him between his head and his heart and his still semi-hard cock. And just then, his cock was losing by only the slimmest of margins. But now that there was maybe something going on around Emma's property, Caine had even more reason to keep his hands and his dick to himself. He needed to figure out if he was right, so he couldn't afford the distraction.

Her eyes snapped back to his, and he didn't want to guess at the emotions running across her pretty face. "Okay, then," she finally said. "Be   safe."

That was his line, but he didn't say it because he didn't want to worry her.

He was plenty good at that all on his own.

And then he didn't know *what* to say. So, with just a nod, he walked out of the kitchen and through the house. "Keep your ears open," he whispered to Chewy, who lifted his little head and wagged his tail as if he understood.

Out at his Harley, Caine gave Emma's street a slow one-eighty scan.

His blood was comprised of at least one part paranoia, so he knew he was more apt than the average bear to see trouble where it didn't exist. Thing was, he wasn't often wrong. Having been a target for trouble from the moment his mother had overdosed on heroin and his father had decided that a five-year-old kid was too great of an inconvenience to deal with, Caine had been raised on identifying and combating trouble.

As he looked at that perfectly quiet street, he felt trouble. He felt hidden eyes and he heard the echo of too-quiet footsteps and he smelled bad intentions heavy and thick on the night air.

And as long as his senses were telling him all of that was true and not just the product of his hyperactive ability to imagine worst-case scenarios, he was going to act like it was true.

Which meant one thing—he needed to surveil Emma Kerry's house. To rule that trouble in or out, once and for all.

Chapter 9

Emma was sitting in the middle of her living floor on Sunday morning amid piles of colorful paper, bows, gift bags, and wrapped presents when the question came to her for maybe the dozenth time.

What the hell happened on Friday night?

One moment, Caine had been all over her, literally devouring her. And the next, there'd been a mile-wide gulf between them.

"We should leave it at that..."

Trying to figure it out had left her distracted all weekend. Not to mention confused, equal parts irritated and hurt, and feeling like somewhere along the way she'd missed something obvious but was being too clueless to know what it was. *Ugh!*

And the frustrating cherry on top was that she couldn't stop thinking about how freaking amazing he'd been. The aggression of his kisses and touch. The surprising fervor with which he'd worshipped her with his mouth. The way he'd tormented her after her orgasm, licking her over-sensitive clit until she thought she'd cry but even then she hadn't wanted it to stop.

The feeling that she could've said or done or admitted to wanting *anything*, and he would've given it to her no questions asked. And, damn, how she'd wanted the opportunity to put that feeling to the test.

The only thing that made any sense to her was that realization she'd made over dinner—that he seemed to be trying to make an argument about why they couldn't work. And if she was right, then perhaps in the cooling off that'd happened while they took Chewy out, dealt with his escape attempt into the alley, and then cleaned up dinner, Caine had revisited that argument. And that time it'd won.

If that's what happened, it didn't bode well for her. Because it meant he'd made up his mind about them, and he'd done it *after* they'd fooled around. Which...*ack!*...really sucked. Especially because her body craved more of what they'd shared. Emma just couldn't stop thinking about how good it'd been, how hard she'd come, and how much she ached for more.

More with him.

Putting the finishing touches on another gift, she wrote *Alison* on a tag and stuck it on the top of the wrapped box. And then she realized she'd been staring at that gift for ten minutes while her mind spun on Caine McKannon.

Man, she needed a distraction, bad. She put the movie *Elf* on while she did the rest of her wrapping, because it was so ridiculous that she could never resist laughing even though it was also really, really stupid.

But at least it pulled her out of her head and she managed not to obsess about her Tall, Dark, and Mysterious Oral Sex God for a few hours. And then she had Alison and her husband to help, too, because she met them at a matinee showing of "The Nutcracker" and then they had dinner afterward.

It was eight o'clock by the time Emma returned home, the night bitter cold but clear. Christmas Eve's Eve. As she sat in her living room, Chewy on her lap, a little pang of sadness squeezed inside her chest. Her grandmother had been such a lively, kick-ass kinda lady. Always cooking and telling stories and wanting to learn new things right up until the end—like the guitar lessons she'd started taking two months before she died because she'd read an article about how playing an instrument helped keep seniors' minds sharp. She was always helping people and had a kind word for everyone she met, whether she knew them or not. She'd always made Christmas so special for Emma, and maybe that's why Em suddenly missed her so bad.

And that little bit of sadness was why Emma called it a day and went to bed before nine o'clock.

She woke up in the middle of the night, unsure what she'd heard but sure she'd heard something. Chewy confirmed it, because he sat alert amid the rumpled covers, his ears perked, his tail giving a few lazy wags. "What was it, boy?"

The dog didn't seem alarmed, so she took some solace in that as she slipped out of bed. The LED screen on her alarm clock read one

AM. She went to the front windows and peered out. Darkness stretched in both directions along the street, interrupted only by circles of light cast by the street lamps and the traffic lights she could just glimpse down at the intersection.

All was quiet.

She went to step back from the window when she saw it. A motorcycle. Parked on the opposite side of the street from her house. Branches from the tree right in front of her house prevented her from seeing it clearly, so she went downstairs, Chewy rushing ahead of her, curiosity making Emma need to know: Was it Caine? And if so, why was he here?

Sure enough, her living room windows gave her a better view. It was Caine's motorcycle, the all-black frame familiar to her from the night he'd sat at her curb, but he was nowhere to be seen. She frowned. What the heck was he doing? It couldn't be coincidence that he was parked near her house, could it?

Thump thump.

Emma froze, and the hair rose up on her arms under the sweatshirt she'd worn to bed. She turned, her gaze raking over dim rooms she knew so well. Padding quietly through the living and dining rooms, she strained to listen. But everything was quiet.

She peered out the dining room window that looked down on the narrow walkway running between her and the next row house, a cut-through from the street to the alley. And then she went to the kitchen and flicked on the back porch light. Nothing.

"What did you expect? Stop freaking yourself out, Em," she said, the sound of her own voice comforting in the quiet.

One last time, she returned to the tight space between the tree and her living room window when her eyes caught movement on the street. A figure with a hood up over his head stepped out of the shadows. The height, the lanky swagger, she knew it was Caine before he even straddled his bike. Her pulse spiked at seeing him, at remembering what they'd done the last time they'd been together, at the mystery of what he was doing *now.*

Of course, her instinct was to go out to him. To ask. To invite him in out of the cold. But she shoved that instinct into a dark room and locked the door. Because she'd been the one to make a move first quite enough. Inviting him in to wait that first night. Getting word to him through Haven and Dare that she wanted to talk. Inviting him to stay for dinner. Flirting with him until he'd let himself off the leash and came at her with all kinds of pent-up want.

Every step of the way had been thrilling.

But after the way he'd left, she didn't want to be the one to put herself out there again. It was his turn to decide he was interested and make a move.

Would he really be out there if he wasn't interested? And if he wasn't interested, what other reason did he have to be hanging out near her house?

Nope. Nopenopenope. She did *not* want to know what was behind door number one or door number two, thank you very much.

So she went back upstairs to bed and pulled the covers over her head, literally and symbolically. And when she woke up on Christmas Eve morning, Caine was gone. Emma had no idea what to think.

Luckily, a day of shopping last-minute Christmas sales with Alison helped take Emma's mind off Caine's strange behavior, at least until Alison asked about him over lunch. Emma hadn't been fully honest, saying only that she'd seen him again when he'd dropped off the cookies. She'd hated holding back on Alison. It was just that Emma was so unclear on exactly what was going on that she wasn't ready to try to explain it. To anyone.

She and Alison emerged from the mall to find big, fat snowflakes falling, the kind you just knew were going to lay. The forecast predicted four to six inches.

"It's gonna be a white Christmas," Emma said, catching a big flake on her tongue as she and Alison made their way to Alison's car.

"Isn't it great? I'm so glad we got Riley his first sled. That'll be so much fun tomorrow."

Alison unlocked the trunk where they stowed their bags, and then they got in the car and waited for it to warm up. "Are you sure you don't want to spend the night?" Alison asked. "We'd love to have you for Christmas morning, too."

Emma shook her head. "I'm sure. You know I appreciate it. But Riley's only five, and Christmas morning is so special at that age. I'll look forward to seeing you all for dinner."

It wasn't the first time Alison had asked, nor the first time Emma had turned her down. She appreciated the invitation, of course, but she didn't want to horn in on their family time that way.

The drive home took a little longer than usual with the roads already getting slippery, but before long, Alison was dropping her at home again. "Merry Christmas, Alison."

"Merry Christmas, Em," Alison said as they hugged over the center console.

"Don't get out," Emma said. "Just pop your trunk so I can grab my things." When she was done, she stood at the curb and waved as Alison pulled away.

Darkness was descending earlier than usual due to the storm, but Emma still took a moment to look up and down her street. Shaking her head at herself, she went inside, where she had to fight her way in against the huge pile of mail that'd been dropped through the slot in her front door.

She kicked off her boots, dropped her bags and purse onto the dining room table, and then went back for the mail, smiling at all the red envelopes that indicated Christmas cards. Feet aching, she half fell into one of the carved chairs at her grandmother's cherished table and worked her way through the dozen or so cards that'd arrived. Photo cards showing friends' children. Holiday letters that caught her up on college classmates' lives. Sparkly cards that left glitter on her fingers.

Emma was enjoying her sparkly hands as she opened the next-to-last red envelope. She pulled the card out. It had a silly cartoon Santa peeking from behind a curtain and read, *You Better Watch Out!*

Snorting, Emma flipped the card open. The interior had the same picture, but focused more tightly on Santa's eyes through the curtain, and it read,

I see you when you're sleeping!
Merry Christmas!

There was no signature. She turned it over and looked at the envelope, but there was no identifying information. Silly kids. How many times had she gotten cards or pictures at school where the kids had forgotten to sign them, and she had to go around asking so she knew who to thank.

The last card had a pretty picture of a church in a snowy field, lights on a small grouping of trees to the side. It was from one of the fifth-grade teachers Emma didn't know well, and she set the envelope aside so she remembered to add the lady's address to her card list for next year.

Chewy paced to the kitchen doorway and gave a little bark. Then two more urgent ones.

"Sorry, sorry," Emma said, retrieving her boots. "I should've taken you out right away, shouldn't I? But Mama's feet hurt, little man."

Chewy's tail beat on a double time, and he began barking and dancing in circles.

"I'm coming, I'm coming," she said, stepping into her boots near the back door. She grabbed a sweatshirt off a hook and slipped into it. "Okay, let's go see how deep the snow is."

Chewy took off like a shot to do his business, but Emma couldn't pay him any mind. Because there were faint footsteps leading from her gate, through her yard, up her steps, and onto her porch. They were recent-ish, judging by how the heavy falling snow had covered and filled them in. But even in the near-dark, she had no doubt that they were definitely there.

Twin reactions erupted inside Emma: anger and fear. The first because someone had trespassed on her property. Had it been Caine? If so, why? The footsteps were under the kitchen window and near the back door. And the second because someone had trespassed on her property. And if it hadn't been Caine, who had it been?

"Come on, Chewy," Emma called. He came right away, a little pile of snow clinging to his black nose. But just then, Emma didn't have time to pay attention to Chewy's cuteness.

Instead, she grabbed her cell phone, fished out the business card from her purse, and dialed Sheriff Martin. It went to voicemail.

Emma left a message. "Hi, Sheriff Martin. This is Emma Kerry. We met last week when there was vandalism at Frederick Elementary. I'm calling to follow up on the conversation we had about my mugging. This might be nothing, but I just found footsteps in my yard and on my porch, congregated near my back door and kitchen window. There's no damage or anything, but after the mugging, I thought I'd let you know. Maybe you could have a patrol or two come by over the next few days? Okay, that's all. Thanks. And Merry Christmas."

She disconnected. And then she realized that her boots were dripping melted snow all over her dining room floor. On a groan, Emma cleaned up and made herself a cup of hot chocolate in an oversized mug so there was plenty of room for the metric-ton of mini-marshmallows she liked to have.

And then she felt at loose ends.

But she wasn't having it. She wasn't letting a little weirdness overshadow her enjoyment of her favorite time of the year. So she put on Christmas carols, lit a few candles, and grabbed some of the chocolate-drizzled caramel popcorn she'd grabbed from the candy store at the mall. She added a few packages to the space under the tree, and then spread out the blanket and a stack of cushy pillows on the floor. The moment she was lying down, the festive tree looming tall in front of her, all felt right in Emma's world. She opened a book on her e-reader, tossed a handful of popcorn in her mouth, and read until her eyelids grew heavy.

She wasn't sure how long she'd been lying there when a plow rumbled past her house, waking her from a little catnap. She stretched against the blanket, accidentally disrupting Chewy, who gave a little groan against her side.

The clock on the wall said that it was quarter 'til ten.

Emma rose and went to the window, curious to see how much snow had fallen. It looked to be a good four or five...

Her mouth fell open. Because there was a motorcycle out there again. Parked a little farther down the block and shrouded in a light gray cover that clung to the bike underneath enough for her to know for sure what it was. Now the question was: whose bike was it? As far as she knew, there was only one biker who'd ever hung around her house...

"What the hell?" she asked, going from sleepy to wound the hell up in about two-point-five seconds. She thought about the tracks on her porch, and that they'd worried her enough to call the sheriff. If that was Caine... She shook her head, anger making her heart beat hard inside her chest. "No, I'm putting an end to this once and for all."

She jammed her feet into her boots, tugged a coat on, and grabbed her phone and keys. "Stay here, Chewy."

Snow fell in fat, wet flakes and crunched under her feet. Emma had no idea where Caine was, but she began looking by going down the little walkway along the side of her house to see if he was in the alley, which was where those footprints in her yard had come from. She thumbed on the flashlight on her phone to guide her way, but found the alley to be empty.

Shining the light on the ground near to her gate, she found lots of footsteps, but then there were more than a few sets all along the alley, which some people used as a short-cut to the next block. She pushed on the gate itself, but the latch held. Reaching over, she wanted to see if she could grab the release mechanism that would allow someone to let themselves in, and she just managed to reach it. She pushed the gate part-way open and peered into her yard.

"Caine? You back here?"

Silence was her only reply. A chill raced down her spine.

On a frown, she closed the gate and squinted against the whirling snow. "Caine?" she called louder. "I know you're here somewhere!" Frustrated, she retraced her steps back up the narrow walkway. At the street, she looked right and left. "Caine?" The wind seemed to swallow her words.

Suddenly, across the street, he stepped out of another walkway like the one right behind her.

Emma didn't hesitate. She marched through the snow—which required not a little effort given the mounds that the plows were already building along the parallel-parked cars—and stalked right up to him. "What are you doing?" she asked.

Just as he said, "What are you doing out here?"

"Since I live here, I'm pretty sure that's *my* question." Her gaze ran over his face, half in shadow under the hood, those icy blue eyes glinting in the street light. He wasn't wearing his Ravens' jacket, but instead some sort of bad-ass-looking black and gray motorcycle coat that made him look like one of the shadow Stormtroopers from the newer Stars Wars movies. She braced her hands on her hips and hated herself a little for noticing how freaking sexy this man was. And for reacting to it, too.

He peered around them. "Emma." His tone was almost as if he were pained.

And that did nothing for the turmoil that had been bubbling up in her gut the past few days. "What? How is you hanging around outside my house every night *leaving it at that*? Isn't that what you said?"

"There's something you need to know." He scrubbed his hands over his face, which was when she noticed that they were bright red and raw.

Concern for him stirred within her, but she was too angry to give it the voice it deserved. "Oh, if it's that you've been prowling around on my back porch, I've seen the footprints in the snow. I'm quite aware, thank you."

A storm rolled in over his expression. If she'd ever thought him intense or intimidating or a little scary, it was nothing compared to how he looked at that moment. He came at her until they were nearly chest to chest. "There are new footprints?"

The agitation rolling off of him took her aback. "Uh, no, not new. I saw them yesterday."

He nodded. "That's what I need to talk to you about." Seriousness. Anger. Regret. Those were what she heard in his voice.

"Tell me," she said, hugging herself against the cold—and against whatever it was he was about to say.

He tucked a strand of her blowing waves behind her ear, and the little touch was so unlike him that she nearly leaned into it. But what she most noticed was how painfully cold his hand was. "Jesus, Caine."

He flinched and yanked his hand back. "Fuck, sorry."

"No, no," she reached for him, and he angled away, his whole posture going rigid. He stuffed his hand in his pocket. She ached at the possibility that he thought she hadn't liked his touch, so she did the touching instead. Slowly, carefully, she took that harsh face in her hands, her thumbs stroking over frozen cheeks, her fingers cradling high, pronounced cheekbones. "How long have you been out here? You're like ice."

His gaze blazed at her. "Doesn't matter. I'm here for however long it takes."

"However long *what* takes?" she asked.

"Catching whoever's been prowling around your house," he said with a swallow that sounded thick and hard, full of regret. "Those weren't my footsteps in your yard and on your porch. My money is on your attacker, and since I let him get away, I'm gonna take care of him. Once and for fucking all."

Emma's heart tripped into a sprint and her belly took a sickly tumble. "You think someone's prowling around my house?"

A single nod. "I didn't leave your kitchen window open, Emma. And someone opened your gate that night that Chewy got out. And in addition to those footsteps..." His hesitation almost killed her, but finally he continued. "...someone tried to break into your basement."

"What?" She whirled and looked at the house, as if a giant neon arrow might suddenly appear to point out all the things that had been done to the place in her absence. But of course, no such signs existed.

And everything looked just like she expected. The big tree in front of the red brick façade of the 1940s-era row house, Christmas lights glowing from the double front windows, the carved wooden door festive with its big, round wreath.

"Through the rear window well," Caine said. "He put the well cover back in place to hide what he'd done, but I found the window broken while you were out on Sunday. The opening was probably too small for a man to get through, though."

Emma could barely process everything Caine was saying. "I...I have to call the police."

"I already have," he said. She peered over her shoulder at him. "Henry Martin is a friend of mine. I know you talked to him. He's apprised of the situation, but he's out of town until Wednesday. In the meantime, I bolted down the well cover and one of Martin's men is riding regular patrols. And I'll be out here watching."

She shook her head. "No, Caine. No, you won't."

Chapter 10

Caine's blood turned to ice as Emma rejected his help. He supposed he deserved that after the way he'd walked out on her the other night, but he wasn't leaving her vulnerable—when it was his failing that had created the vulnerability in the first place.

"Emma, I know I fucked up in how I treated you. But you need to hear me. I'm not leaving."

"Okay, fine. I hear you. But hear *me*. You're not staying out here while you do it." She arched a brow over those warm blue eyes.

He frowned. "Meaning?"

She tilted her head like he was confusing her. Which, right back at ya. "Meaning you're coming in. If you're going to keep an eye out for this guy for me, then you're not going to stand in a snowstorm 'til your skin turns red and raw to do it. On Christmas Eve, no less. You're coming in the damn house."

He inhaled to—

"Don't even think of saying no. You *are* the kind of person who gets invited in, Caine. At least, you are to *me*."

If she'd sucker punched him, it wouldn't have stolen his breath as much as throwing his words back at him managed to do. And *damn* if her words weren't pinballing around in his chest, knocking against things that didn't often get disturbed. But he couldn't think about that just then. "Em—"

She gasped and her eyes went wide. "Oh, my God. Caine. *Oh, my God.*"

Alarm lanced through his blood. "What? What is it?"

"You have to see something," she said, already moving to cross the street. "Oh, my God."

He was at her back in an instant. And then they were in her house and stepping across a pile of pillows and blankets. She beelined for the dining room table, Chewy excitedly in tow, and roughly sorted through a stack of mail.

"Look," she said, turning with a piece of paper in hand. No, a card.

The glassy fear in her eyes just about gutted him. And then he looked at the card.

You Better Watch Out! a Peeping Tom Santa said. On the inside, that same Santa proclaimed, *I see you when you're sleeping!* It was unsigned.

What. The. Fuck. Seriously. What kind of twisted company made a card for Christmas that was this goddamned creepy?

"Is there an envelope?" he asked, rage rearing up like a beast inside his chest.

"Yeah," she said, her voice no more than a whisper. "Here."

Her name and address had been printed on a label, and there was no return address. "The stamp hasn't been cancelled."

"What?"

He turned it so she could see. "It hasn't been cancelled. There's no postmark. This wasn't delivered by the mailman, Emma."

Her eyes went wide. "Someone dropped it through my door. Personally."

Trouble stalked around inside Caine's lizard brain. The part of him that was all instinct, the part where fight and flight and the will for survival lived. And Caine knew. Emma didn't just have a prowler. Or an intruder. Emma had a fucking stalker.

"Someone's watching me?" Her inflection posed it as a question, but she was already nodding to herself, working it out just as Caine had. Fingers pressed to her mouth, she started shaking her head. "Oh, Jesus. This might be even bigger…" Her gaze collided with his. "Someone threw a brick through the window of my classroom at school. The weekend you and I met. I got to school on Monday morning to discover the vandalism. Do you…do you think that's part of this?"

Aw, fucking hell. Alarm bells blared inside his brain. Yeah, there was *every goddamned chance* that was part of this.

"Don't hold back on me, Caine. Not about this," she said.

"Maybe it's better not to hide from the truth?"

"*Always,*" he'd told her just moments after he'd broken into her house for her.

God, she was brave. He knew firsthand how hard it was to live knowing your life might be in danger. And to face that danger head on. So he respected the hell out of the way she was handling this. "Given everything I now know, I think it's too coincidental not to be related."

She released a shaky breath and nodded. "Okay. Okay."

"And, if I'm going to take this to the logical conclusion," Caine said, seeing this whole thing laid out from start to finish for the very first time. Sonofabitch. Why hadn't he put it all together sooner? "I'm going to have to say that your mugging wasn't any coincidence either." And that meant that all of this really was his fault. Because if he'd done what he should've that first night, none of the rest of this escalation ever would've happened. "Fuck. It's entirely possible the man wasn't trying to grab your purse, Emma."

She put a hand to her forehead and rubbed. "So, if he wasn't trying for my purse…"

He could tell from her tone that she *knew*—*she* was what her attacker had really been after. But she'd asked that he not hold back, so he wasn't going to. *Does that apply to how much you want to touch her again, McKannon? Or how sick your stomach's been with regret since you cut and run? Or how fucking impossible it was to avoid thinking of her these past days? You gonna come clean with all of that, too?* None of which he could deal with now. Not when this thing was so much bigger than he even knew.

"I think he was trying to take you," he said. Protective rage roared through Caine so hard and so fast that it was like his blood was suddenly made of gasoline. All at once, the combination of his winter outer riding gear with a sweatshirt and a base layer was too much, and he ripped the coat off and hung it over a chair. "Sonofabitch," he growled. Why hadn't he seen this sooner?

"Wow. Okay." Her lips trembled, but she was holding herself together like a champ.

"Do you have any enemies, Emma? An ex-boyfriend? Someone that seemed put out that you rejected him? Anything like that?"

Her gaze went distant, but finally she shook her head. "Not that I can think of. The last guy I dated moved to DC in August, and it was his idea to break up because he was moving. It was amicable."

Caine's mind raced. "What about people you see hanging around the neighborhood, the intersection? Men who might hang at that convenience store and maybe could figure out your routine?" Although, he had to admit, while they'd been surveilling Ana Garcia's house, they hadn't seen anything like that, and they would've noticed.

"Sometimes there's a homeless man who pushes a big grocery cart of his belongings down the alley out back, but he's never said a word to me. And everyone who's ever mentioned him has described him as harmless."

Blowing out a breath, Caine made mental notes about all these possibilities, but his gut wasn't yet feeling pulled by any of them.

She pressed her hands together as if she were praying and rested them against her chin. "So, what then? What do I do?"

"*We*," he said as an urgent, demanding possessiveness dug its claws into his soul. Dug them in, *deep*.

And it was, without question, something he'd never felt before in his whole life. When you felt as unworthy as he did, you rarely believed that you deserved to possess anything at all. But now, in the face of her vulnerability, Caine dared to hope that he might deserve...what? Not *her*, exactly, because after being viewed as no more than a possession by the couple that ran his group home, the idea of possessing another person made his stomach roll. But maybe the chance to get to know her, at the very least. And maybe even the chance to give her the things he'd always wanted but had never been able to have.

Even daring to hope for such things made him feel like the bottom might fall right out from underneath him. And when that happened, he'd just fall and fall and fall...

But if she was going to be brave, he sure the fuck would, too. "We'll figure this out, Emma. Do you hear me? You're not in this alone." His voice sounded like it'd been scoured with sandpaper.

She peered up at him, and her bottom lip trembled a little more. "Promise?"

"Jesus, come here," he rasped, hauling her in against his chest. He held her tight with one arm and stroked her hair back with the other. And Christ, she felt so good there. So warm and soft against all his cold hardness. So right. These thoughts were so foreign to him he hardly knew what to do with them, but that didn't make them any less true. He had to swallow around a knot of emotion before he could go on, but when he finally did, his voice was rock solid again. "I give you my word, Emma."

He made one more promise, too, but this one he kept to himself. Once, he'd failed to protect someone he should've. Worse than that, her death had been his fault.

Caine vowed to himself—he wouldn't make the same mistake twice.

This time, he'd rather die first.

* * * *

"Are you sure you'll be okay here?" Emma asked, hardly able to believe…well, so many things, really. Because the night had been one long tidal wave of revelations that left her feeling like she could barely keep her head above water. But, for the current moment, what she almost couldn't believe was that Caine was sitting on her couch preparing to spend the night in her house.

For one moment, earlier, she'd thought he was leaving, but he'd only gone outside long enough to move his bike off the street to the where the cut-through walkway met the alley behind her house.

So now, she *had* to believe that he was going to be there for her. Not only because he'd been there for her even when she hadn't realized it, but also because the promise he'd made to her had been said with so much conviction that even now just the memory of it rushed goosebumps over her skin.

"You're not in this alone. I give you my word."

"More than," he said, tugging the knit hat off his head and scrubbing at his short black hair. He tossed the hat aside. "I don't require a lot, Emma. Don't feel like you have to take care of me."

The words made her ache. Because she didn't think anyone took care of Caine McKannon. Worse, she feared that quite possibly no one had *ever* taken care of him. She didn't know how that could be, but something about him set off the same alarm inside her that rang whenever one of her kids was in some kind of trouble at home.

Nodding, she turned to go upstairs, but then she turned back. Maybe because he was *here* for her. Maybe because it was Christmas Eve. Maybe because something about this man spoke to something inside Emma. And she said, "What if I want to take care of you?"

That pale gaze cut up to her. Narrowed. Flashed hot. "Night, Emma," he said.

She heard the command behind it, so she turned and padded up the steps, Chewy at her side.

But three hours later, she remained wide awake. The snow storm sent wind battering ominously against the windows. Every once in a while, something banged somewhere outside, sending her heart into a desperate sprint. The old house creaked and groaned, and her brain was convinced that every noise was her attacker closing in on her.

Not even Chewy's calm slumber was enough to convince her there was nothing to worry about.

"Screw it," Emma said, suddenly sitting up in bed. She grabbed a pillow and the weighted fleece blanket off her footboard. "Come on, Chewchew." She scooped him up so his hopping strides down the steps wouldn't disturb Caine. "We gotta be quiet, okay?"

Out into the hall. Down the steps. Into the living room, still illuminated by the warm rainbow of lights on the tree.

"What's wrong?" Caine asked, propping himself up on one elbow.

"I'm sorry to wake you," she said. Even though his company made her feel better. A lot better. "I couldn't sleep." She put Chewy down and arranged her pillow and blanket, then she stretched out on her back.

"You're not serious right now, right?" he said from right above her.

She looked up to find him peering over the edge of the couch. "What?"

"I'm not sleeping on the couch while you're on the floor."

"I've slept here many times. I don't mind."

He sighed. "*Emma.*"

"Don't be difficult, Caine." She yawned.

He chuffed out a little laugh, and it made her smile. Especially when he leaned over the couch again. "No one besides my brothers has ever given me as much shit as you do."

"Is that a good thing or a bad thing?" she asked, even though his tone had mostly sounded amused, if not a little exasperated.

"I'm not sure yet," he said.

She laughed. "Well, I don't know what to tell you, Caine. You're not that scary. And I get the impression that you need someone to give you a little shit every now and again," she teased.

He turned so that he lay on his stomach, half his shoulder hanging off the couch. One hand came down and stroked a path through the length of her hair. "I don't want to scare you at all, Emma."

Aw, God, the sincerity in his voice reached inside her chest and took root there. "You make me feel safe," she said.

"I…" He shook his head and cleared his throat. "I can't lay up here while you're down there," he said again.

"Then…then come down. If you want." Her heart thundered in her chest, because she really wanted. Not just because his proximity made her feel safer, but because she'd been craving closeness with him ever since he'd walked out of her kitchen that night. Closeness of any kind. Of every kind.

For a moment, he didn't react at all, and then he pushed himself up, stepped over her, and stretched out on the blanket an arm's reach away. Emma worked hard to act nonchalant and keep her utter exhilaration off her face. A feat that was easier when Chewy lumbered out of his dog bed to sniff Caine—his socks, his threadbare jeans, the old white undershirt. Caine laughed—he actually *laughed*—when Chewy got to his face and sniffed, then licked at the thin growth of scruff that covered his jaw.

"The floor is his territory," Emma said, grinning as she watched Caine tolerate her best friend. "This is the official welcome."

"That right?" Caine asked, petting Chewy's back once, twice. Gingerly, like he wasn't sure if he might hurt him.

Emma nodded against her pillow, her heart doing a little flip-flop in her chest. "Consider yourself officially adopted as one of Chewy's human staff members. He will now expect you to feed him, fill his water dish, give him T-R-E-A-Ts, take him for walks, and do other tasks as assigned by the management."

"T-R-E-A-Ts?" Caine repeated, amusement plain in his tone.

"I'm too comfortable to get up to get him one, but if I say the word, he'll bug me until I do. Thus, the highly secret code of spelling the word instead."

Chewy made his way back to his dog bed and laid down with a huff and a long groan.

"Same, Chewy," Caine said.

As Emma watched the interaction, observing Caine's gentle kindness toward the most important creature in her life, those roots in her chest began to grow.

"I was scared," she whispered. "Upstairs."

Caine came closer. "I'm so fucking sorry."

She rolled onto her side, coming closer, too. "You're here, Caine. That counts for a lot. No, that counts for everything. You have no reason to be sorry."

Something flashed behind his eyes, something that said he didn't agree. But he didn't voice it. For a long moment, he just stared at her. And it was quite possibly one of the most intimate moments of Emma's life. Lying in the darkness early on Christmas morning, walls and barriers down so that another person could look into her eyes and see everything she was, everything she wanted, and everything she feared.

Gathering her courage, she forced out the words that told him what she most wanted just then. "Can I lay close to you?"

He groaned and pulled her to him, and then he rolled onto his back so that she was sprawled all along his side, her head on his chest, his arm holding her tight. "I'll give you anything I can, Emma."

She hugged herself to his chest, feeling for the first time just how markedly lean he was. "Right now, I just want you, Caine. That's more than enough."

Chapter 11

Caine didn't sleep. Didn't move. Nearly didn't breathe.

Because he'd never before allowed another person to sleep with him this way. As a boy, he'd had to share a bedroom with other boys, sure. But at no point in the seventeen years since his fourteen-year-old self had run from that home had Caine ever done this.

His wakefulness now wasn't because he was uncomfortable, though. Instead, it was because this moment, *this...connection?* felt so pure, so comforting, so fundamentally good that he didn't want to miss a single moment.

In what little heart he still possessed, he knew whatever this was wasn't likely to last. *Daring to hope* didn't mean truly believing that a nearly impossible situation would work out the way he wanted. That wasn't life's M.O., at least not in his experience. Not ever.

But Emma made him want to *try*. To hope. To take the risk, no matter how many pieces he'd shatter into if it all went to shit. Scratch that. *When*. When it all went to shit.

In the meantime, he was going to memorize every second of *good* he got, in case he never got any more.

Breathing in the scent of strawberries from Emma's hair, Caine made a mental catalogue of all this good. The slow, regular beat of her heart against his ribs. The heat of her everywhere they touched. The little twitches of her fingers against his chest. The deep, even draws of her breathing. That he could touch her hair and her shoulder and her arm as much as he wanted, and when she reacted at all, it was only to burrow in tighter against him.

Outside of fucking and the occasional handshake, Caine rarely touched another person or allowed himself to be touched. More often than not in his life, touch had been a painful thing. Hateful and hurtful and mean. So, just as he'd done with food and sleep and relationships, he'd shied away from touch, shied away so much that he sometimes wondered if he existed at all. If no one ever touched him, how could they know if he was real? Maybe people were all just twisted figments in each other's tortured imaginations.

And that kind of jacked-up thinking was just one of the many reasons why all this might fit squarely into the category of *felt good but was a really fucking bad idea.*

"Then why are you doing it?" he whispered into the still of the night.

Because Emma was the first person who'd truly seen Caine in *years*. Not the biker. Not the ruthless enforcer of rules and dispenser of justice. Not the ink-and-piercing-covered punk. Each one of those personas its own kind of armor against the darkest sides of life.

But Emma...somehow it was like Emma had looked behind the veil. And, God help him, but it seemed like she hadn't recoiled at the glimpse of the real him that she'd gotten. She treated him like he was normal, like he was her equal, like he was worthy of her respect. She made him fucking *laugh*. And, in such a short amount of time, she made him want, and hope, and care. It was almost as if being in her presence was like being pulled out of the darkness into her light, like being plugged into the world of the living, instead of floating as nothingness in the realm of ghosts that he so often inhabited.

Oh, there was *more* for her yet to see. She had no idea about the dirtiest, filthiest parts of him. He was going to have to tell her, and there was every likelihood that all this goodness would end right then.

But in the meantime, he committed every shred of this to memory.

On a sigh that sounded like pure contentment, Emma drew herself closer, her face slipping in against his neck, her thigh sliding to rest high up on his.

Caine was hard in a fucking instant. Because *now* he had some new things to add to that catalogue. The way her leg nudged against his balls. And the tight press of her core against the muscles of his thigh. And then, *Jesus Christ*, she whimpered in her sleep and her hand fisted in his shirt. A breath shuddered out of her. Caine held her tighter, unsure if she was having a nightmare but wanting her to remember that he was there. Just like he'd promised to be.

By the time the first gray light of dawn crept into the room, Caine was struggling against the leaden weight of his eyelids. He yawned so wide his jaw cracked.

Emma stirred against him, her lips pressing to his neck.

He groaned at the sweetness of it, and at the fact that he'd been hard so much overnight that he was strung fucking tight.

"Merry Christmas," Emma whispered, not otherwise moving.

Caine debated how to respond. Christmas wasn't something he usually recognized. It'd been a source of torment for him as a child, so as an adult, he'd never seen the point. But he knew it was important to her. One look at this house proved that.

"Yeah, it just might be," he managed. And then he went one step further, giving her a piece of himself that he'd never before given anyone. "It's already the best Christmas morning I've ever had."

"Nothing's happened yet," she said, a soft, sleepy humor in the words.

"Not true. I got to hold you." His heart beat harder at the admission.

"That is…the sweetest thing anyone has ever said to me."

"I'm not sweet, Emma."

She shifted so that her chin rested on the center of his chest, more of her body coming up on more of his. "You're not *only* sweet, but you are absolutely capable of sweetness and gentleness."

Fuck, what pretty words, even though they painted such a false picture of him. And *fuuck*, what a pretty face staring back at him, so soft and affectionate and open. "I'm not a hero, Emma. You need to remember that."

She gave him an appraising look, one he feared was too observant, too insightful. "A hero is merely someone who risks himself in some way to help others, even if he's scared of taking that risk or putting himself out there for others. By that definition…" She reached for his face and traced patterns over his skin. Around his jaw, his eye, his mouth. And then her fingers pushed into his short hair, her fingertips scratching against his scalp so good he nearly groaned.

All he could do was shake his head. She had it all wrong. All wrong about him, anyway. *Tell her.*

But before he could, Emma shifted again, bringing her face closer to his. Close enough that if he just leaned up, he could have a taste of her again. "You know what you are?"

Yeah. Yeah, he really fucking did. A jagged boulder slid into his gut. But he wanted to hear what she had to say. "What?"

"You're the man who risked himself and saved me, we now know, from being dragged away to God only knows what fate." She blew out a shaky breath, and damn if her fear didn't reach into his rib cage and make it hard to breathe. Or maybe what invaded his chest was his own fear—at realizing how close he'd been to losing Emma Kerry before he'd ever met her at all. White-hot anger lanced through him at the thought.

"Okay," he said.

"I'm not done." She pressed a soft kiss against his lips, and the freeness of her affection stunned him. "You're also the man who recognized that I was in danger and took it upon himself to watch over me and my house, to even talk to the police about it."

He shrugged with one shoulder, his gaze falling somewhere in between them. "Providing protection, investigating threats, and installing security, this is what I do for the Ravens. I know you don't know a lot about us, but we have a whole mission around defending people who can't defend themselves. So I just slipped into that mode. But I should've told you what was going on. I just... I didn't want to worry you until I was sure. And I didn't—*fuck*, I know this was selfish— but I didn't want you to hate me for letting the guy get away."

"Yeah, you should've told me. So I could be more aware and know I might need to defend myself. Look at me," she said, tilting her face to try to align their gazes.

He lifted his and met those warm blues head on, ready for whatever criticism and anger she wanted to dish out.

"But last night, out on the street, you admitted you had something to tell me. And then you did. Just...next time, maybe tell me at the start, okay?"

Caine blinked. That was it?

"And if you have any advice on how to make my voice louder or more convincing than the one in your head that keeps telling you I could ever hate you or that anything about my attack was your fault, could you please let me know?"

His jaw dropped, and Caine felt like he'd just walked cartoon-like into an unseen pole. *This*...this was just one more proof that this woman *saw* him. Right now, that wasn't super fucking comfortable. But it was so foreign to be seen that he couldn't do anything but bask in it, even if he felt utterly exposed.

"Fuck, Emma," he managed, his thoughts too tangled to even attempt a meaningful answer to her question. "What are you doing to me?"

"Trying to let you know I care," she said. Like it was obvious. Like it was normal. Like it wasn't blowing his goddamn mind. And then she just kept right on doing it. "Because you're also the man who, for almost three weeks now, has inhabited my dreams and dominated my thoughts and..." She ducked her gaze.

"What?" he rasped, dying for her to continue. He rolled them, pinning her under him. And, damn if that wasn't a heady thing, especially as she went soft and pliant, her cheeks filling with a pink heat he tasted with his tongue. "And what?"

"And made me so horny so often that I feel like I'm going a little crazy."

Trapped in between them, his cock was so demandingly hard that his hips surged against hers. "Christ," he bit out, half wondering if he was asleep in his trailer having a dream from which he never wanted to wake. Because stuff like this didn't happen to him. "I'll get you off again. Gladly. Did you like my mouth?"

Her eyes went wide. "I freaking loved your mouth. Did you really need to ask?"

"I just want to be good for you."

"Then just be you. I'm crazy about that mouth, but I'm also crazy about the rest of you, too." Her arms looped around his neck and her fingers played in the back of his hair. It was only a matter of time... Her fingers moved over the ruined skin above his hairline where the hair didn't grow right anymore. She didn't say anything about it, but he didn't miss the questions that passed over her expression. "Kiss me?"

On a groan, he did. His mouth found hers already open, her tongue meeting his lick for lick and stroke for stroke. She moaned and shifted beneath him, her knees pulling up and opening so that his hardness lined up with her sweet heat. They kissed until he couldn't breathe and didn't want to, not if it meant parting from her, and then she rolled her hips and ground her core against him. Once, twice, three times. God, she could use him like this forfuckingever and he'd die a happy man. Or as close to happy as he was capable of. "Yeah, Emma. You want to get off on my cock?"

Her eyes were soft and hooded and so full of desire that he thrust himself and met her hips as they rolled again. "Yes," she whispered, panting against his lips. "I told you. I want you. All of you."

The words chased away some of the lust-drunk haze in his brain. He pulled back from the kiss. He wasn't shy about sex. Like, not at all. But he was usually with people who he'd made prior arrangements with through hook-up message boards, and therefore whose whole approach to sex was transactional and purely physical. Fucking was a given before anyone even walked in the room. This...this was different. And the unknown expectations and boundaries were suddenly kinda fucking terrifying. "What do you want, Emma? You're gonna have to spell it out for me. I don't want to risk reading you wrong."

She cupped his face in her hand. "I want you inside me."

Jesus. His forehead fell against hers as he was torn in two. Between wanting nothing more than what she wanted and being dead sure he shouldn't take it. "Are you sure? There's so fucking much you don't know about me."

She shook her head. "Listen to *my* voice, Caine. I want you. I ache for you. And I know everything I need to know to make this decision. Unless...unless you don't want this with me?"

"No," he bit out, thrusting the hard length of his cock against her soft heat. "Fuck, no, that's not it. Tell me you can't feel how much I want you."

Her fingers tugged at the back of his shirt. "So then—"

He pushed up on his hands, separating them and halting her effort to undress him. Regret slinked through his gut, and he wondered if this would be the moment she came to her senses. "Wait," he said, getting up to stand on the blanket.

She sat up as Caine undressed down to his badly ruined birthday suit, revealing another layer of what was so fucking ugly about him. His dick went soft in anticipation of her revulsion. He'd seen it on others' faces before, despite that his profile on the boards was brutally, graphically honest about everything he was and wasn't.

Finally he met her wide eyes. "You can change your mind."

Emma shifted to her knees as her gaze ran over him, no doubt taking in everything. On his front, the scars, the cigarette burns, the tattoos, the piercings. And then he turned and gave her his back. Where fire had ravaged the right side with second- and third-degree burns from the bottom of his ribs to the lower part of his scalp. He'd inked parts of that skin, which was whiter and stretched tighter from the skin grafts and surgeries, but not all of it.

"Come closer." Warily, he stood in front of where she now knelt. And then she wrapped her arms around his ass and laid the side of her face against his lower belly. "I want you inside me."

The words hit him like a shock wave, nearly taking him right off his feet. His heart tripped over itself. His cock grew. The backs of his eyes stung. Blinking up at the ceiling, his hand fell to Emma's hair, the strokes against the silky blond the only thing he could manage for a long moment.

And then, *Jesus*, her tongue bathed his erection. Caine nearly doubled over from the unexpected goodness of it, especially since his reaction apparently fueled her on. She gave another, wetter, lick along his whole length and then took him inside her mouth.

"*Em*," he rasped, peering down at the sight of her on her knees, at his feet, with his cock in her mouth. Both of his hands fell to her head. She peered up at him, so much emotion in those blue eyes. But he couldn't guess at it. He could only feel. It was a sweet, sweet torture, especially as his hips wanted to take over, wanted to swing free.

How is this happening?

Her arms smoothed up his back, her left hand lightly caressing his burn scar before she pulled away, her hand and her mouth. "Can I touch your scars? I mean, will it hurt if I do? I want to touch you everywhere, but I don't want to hurt you."

He did go to his knees then. Caine took her face in his hands and kissed her like she was water and he'd been thirsting to death all his life. Occasionally, someone asked him if his back still hurt him. Usually after sex as he dressed to leave. He always said *no*, even though the phantom pain caused by destroyed nerves sometimes hurt so much he couldn't sleep. But no one had ever asked his permission or sought his guidance the way Emma just had. "You can touch me," he said around the edge of the kiss, "but I know how fucking ugly it is."

She gasped. "Caine, no, I think you're—"

"I wish I had so much more to offer you," he went on.

"You're amazing, Caine. I want to explore every inch of you."

He growled. "Don't lie to me."

Emma reared back. "I'm not. You need to hear me. *Believe* me." She pulled off her sweatshirt and the little cotton T-shirt beneath it. And then pushed down the thin sleep shorts and yellow satin panties until she was naked too.

And God. *Goddamn.* She was so pretty and perfect that Caine could hardly look at her. But he did look. At the tumble of her blond waves against her fair skin. At the erect nipples on her small breasts. At how the indent of her waist flared out at her hips. At the dark-blond triangle he'd seen before. He didn't deserve her, but Christ help him, he wanted her. His cock jutted out between them, arousal coating the tip.

She laid herself out in front of him, knees bent, legs parted. "Let me show you that you're enough just as you are, Caine. Be with me."

Chapter 12

Emma's heart felt like it might explode right out of her chest. From the ache of the way Caine had revealed himself to her and the injuries he'd endured. From the anticipation of being with him and the hope that he might believe her body even more than her words. From the expansive warmth of realizing that she was in deeper with this man than she'd admitted to herself.

Way deeper. How had that happened so fast?

"I want you," she said, refusing to analyze it in that moment. It just *was*, and for now, that was all that mattered. "I have condoms upstairs in the bathroom medicine cabinet unless you have some?"

"I got it," he said, reaching for his jeans. He withdrew his wallet and then a condom packet from within. Watching him roll it on sent a shot of electricity through her belly. His cock was long and curved with a thick head. He took himself in hand, stretched out over her, and looked her in the eye. "I want you, too, but it would kill me if you regretted this."

God, what had happened to him that made him say such a thing? From all appearances, Caine McKannon was intimidating and tough and hard, but Emma wondered how much of that was protection for some unhealed wound inside him. "Feel how wet I am, Caine."

His fingers fell between her legs, stroking through her arousal. His middle finger penetrated her, and they both moaned as he stroked in and out. "You're so fucking perfect."

She arched at the teasing promise of his touch. "I'm just a normal girl, trying to seduce a boy."

A freaking *amazing* boy. She hadn't lied about that. Caine was an artist's canvas come to life, with possibly more of his skin covered in ink than not. Abstract designs, single words and longer quotes she hadn't yet read, a pair of angel wings over his heart with the word *Grace*. And so many others. He'd used some of his tattoos to cover scars—she could already see that. And then there were the piercings—little black spikes through his nipples, silver balls that appeared to be connected on either side of his clavicle bones, and a silver circle through his scrotum right below the base of his cock.

And she thought she'd been fascinated before…

The side of his mouth drew up, and the lopsided smile he gave her after all that seriousness filled her chest with a warm pressure. "Consider me seduced." Kneeling between her thighs, he lined his cock up with her opening and slowly, so slowly, sank deep. "Jesus, Emma, to be inside you," he rasped, holding himself still.

The raw pleasure on his face ratcheted up her arousal as she threw her head back and breathed through the amazing fullness of his invasion. It'd been five months since she'd last had sex with her summer fling, who'd moved to DC. "It's so good, Caine."

He withdrew almost to the tip before pushing back in. "Fuck, that looks amazing. My cock sliding into you." He repeated the strokes, his gaze glued to the spot where their bodies met, his hands going to her thighs to push her open.

On a moan, she peered up at him, her gaze dragging over new details she noticed of his body. His stomach was hard and flat, the contour of his ribs was visible on his sides, and his broad shoulders and thicker biceps were more cut than he was elsewhere. His collar and hip bones were also visible. He possessed a hunger-pang frame full of hard planes and rough edges, and with every thrust, his muscles flexed in the most amazing way. Emma couldn't wait to feel him lie atop her, but she was in no hurry to lose this view. "I feel the same way about seeing you above me while you're holding me open and buried deep inside me."

A visible shudder went through him, and knowing he was as worked up as she was spiraled sensation down her spine and low into her belly. His arms almost trembled as he took her in deliciously slow, grinding strokes that bottomed out inside her each and every time. He trembled as if he was holding himself back.

"I want whatever you want, Caine," she said.

His gaze collided with hers, and those eyes were white-blue fire.

"Everything about me is hard," he gritted out.

"Show me," she said.

"*Fuck.*" He came down on her then, one of his arms hooked under her knee, the other wrapping around her neck in a tight hold he used as leverage for an absolutely breath-stealing pounding. His hips snapped against her skin hard and fast enough that she expected bruises from his hip bones. His pubic bone crashed into her clit again and again, driving her wild. And those eyes blazed into her very soul.

Emma came. The orgasm detonated with a suddenness that made her whole body go rigid and shake. She clung to him as his cock moved in her, drawing out her pleasure until her vision went fuzzy around the edges.

"Christ, that was the sexiest thing I've ever seen," he said, his voice full of gravel. "Gonna make me come too fast."

"Want you to come," Emma managed, her heart a freight train in her chest.

Caine's mouth fell on hers in an aggressive, demanding kiss. And then he changed positions, pressing her wrists to the floor, holding himself above her, and penetrating her with hammering, punctuated thrusts that moved them across the blanket and, impossibly, stirred arousal within her core again.

He knocked Emma's breath out of her on every stroke until she was crying out and straining and writhing in a rhythm that matched his movements. No one had ever taken her this hard, and the intensity of it was a mind-blowing revelation. Being twenty-seven and single meant that Emma had a collection of vibrators, porn clips, and erotic novels that got regular use. She'd always been drawn to depictions of rough sex, but never before found someone who could do more than play at it. Now, she knew for sure—she got off on it as much in real life as in fantasy.

Got off on it *hard*.

"Caine, God, I'm…gonna…"

"Fuck, yeah." His grip tightened on her wrists and his hips smacked her clit faster. "Come on me again."

The words finished winding her up, up, up and then she was gasping out his name while her hips shuddered and her thighs shook.

Caine's whole weight fell on her and his hands found tight purchase against her skin. He roared his release against her neck, his hips jerking as his cock pulsed inside her. It seemed to go on and on until the sounds that ripped from his throat were almost tortured. Emma wrapped her arms around his shoulders and head and held him through it.

In truth, the power of what they'd shared left her head spinning, and she needed the holding, too.

* * * *

"Aaaah, what the hell?" Caine yelled, flinching.

Chewy sniffed them and whined pitifully, clearly feeling neglected. Emma burst out laughing. "He wanted to play, too."

"He licked my ass."

Emma laughed harder. "He...he has...good taste," she gasped out around the laughter.

Caine's whole face cranked into a frown. When he spoke, it was to the dog. "That's not cool, man."

Now tears gathered in her eyes and she kicked her feet against the floor as her amusement stole her breath, especially when Chewy sat and tilted his head at Caine.

She pressed a hand over her mouth as the hilarity of the moment crashed into how overwhelming the sex had been and snowballed into an overload of emotion. "Sorrysorry," she said, trying but failing to get herself under control.

Caine pulled her hand away and pressed it to the floor again. His eyes were more open, more clear, more at ease than she'd ever seen them before. "I rarely make anyone laugh or smile, so please don't hide it from me. It's fucking beautiful."

Oh, my heart.

Here he was, this man with so many rough edges—and certainly some about which she didn't yet know, judging by what he'd said earlier—but he came at her with this aching sweetness. Again and again.

"So sweet to me," she said.

He released her wrist, then lifted it, looking. "What we did just now, that wasn't sweet. Did I... I didn't hurt you, did I?"

"Hey," she said, grasping his face and making him look at her. "No, it was the opposite of hurt, believe me. I asked you to show me what you like, and you did. And I came so hard I thought I was going to pass out. Twice. All of that was freaking *sweet*." That reserved seriousness was returning to his expression and his eyes again, as if someone was lowering the blinds over his soul. And it made her need to know. "Was it okay for you?"

"Christ, Emma, it's still blowing my fucking mind." Warmth flooded through her, and then he rolled off of her, his hand catching and fisting the condom. "Mind if I use the bathroom?" he asked.

"My house is absolutely your house, Caine." She smiled. "Top of the steps."

He gave her his back as he stepped into his jeans. In the morning light, the skin that'd been burned stood out more starkly than it had in the dimness. She couldn't imagine how much a burn of that size must've hurt, and wondered if he'd be willing to talk about what'd happened. He made for the stairs without another word, and Emma stretched against the blanket like a cat in the sun. And then an idea struck her.

She threw on her sweatshirt and panties, rushed to the dining room closet, and rooted around for something that might be right, or at least funny, or even hilariously terrible. She used this closet to store gift wrap, craft supplies, and things she picked up that might make good gifts or classroom prizes or that she just liked and didn't know what to do with until the right moment or person came along. But her closet was failing her now, and it made her stomach squeeze. Because there was no way she wasn't figuring out something for Caine to open as a gift on Christmas morning.

Rushing water that told her he'd flushed the toilet sounded from the ceiling, and she skidded into the kitchen, her thoughts spinning as she opened the pantry...and landed on a case of the orange soda Caine seemed to like.

"That's stupid," she said, right before she grabbed the cardboard handle of the six-pack of bottles and returned to the gift closet. She found a decorative bag big enough for the soda, and stuffed it with red and green paper. She'd just scrawled his name on a tag when footsteps sounded from the top of the steps. Heart pounding, she dropped the gift bag at the tree just as Caine stepped in from the foyer.

He gave her such a suspicious look that she could only chuckle. "Morning," she said, brazening it out.

He nodded. "Everything okay?"

She moved to him, slowly, uncertainly, and stopped just short of touching him. "Yes. You?"

A single nod. His expression remained full of suspicion. "Yeah."

"Um, we're not gonna be weird now, are we?" she asked. Because she figured, if so, it was better to just get that whole situation out of the way, seeing as it was Christmas freaking Day and all.

He chuffed out a little laugh. With one hand, he grasped her by the neck and pulled her in against his bare chest. "Weird is kinda SOP for me, Emma, but you just keep calling me on it when it gets to be too much."

Her arms went around him and she nuzzled his chest and breathed him in. He smelled faintly of soap, and more strongly of sex and her and the two of them together. She dragged her nose along his skin on a deep inhale, wanting to drink him in. When she neared his nipple, she flicked his piercing with her tongue.

He sucked in a sharp breath.

"Sorry. Couldn't resist," she said, peering up at him.

His mouth came down on hers. The kiss was deep and lingering. When he pulled back he shook his head. "Never apologize for that."

She smiled. "I have to take Chewy out and then I'll make us some breakfast."

"I can take him out," he said. "I want to do a quick walk around anyway."

Her gut dropped at the reminder of the reality that had thrown them together in the first place. But she also wanted to enjoy this day with him, and for him to enjoy it, too. "Okay. Any requests for Christmas morning breakfast? Do you fall more in the bacon-sausage-eggs protein camp or the pancakes-waffles-toast carbs camp?"

"If I eat it's usually just an apple, so anything you make will be special." He gave her another lingering kiss. And then he swiped his shirt off the floor and crossed to where the rest of his things were folded. "I need you to know something and I don't want you to be alarmed," he said, tugging clothing over his head. First, a form-fitting black Under Armour shirt that looked really freaking sexy. Then the white tee and black hoodie.

"Um, okay?"

Caine picked up a pair of black Under Armour pants. Beneath lay a handgun in a small holster. "Just to be on the safe side," he said. "And in case you're wondering, I have a permit for it." He held it up to show her, and then he slid it into his jeans at the small of his back. It attached with a clip.

Her pulse kicked up. Because a gun brought home just how potentially dangerous this situation was. A man had tried to grab her. Knew where she lived and worked. And had violated both of those spaces in one way or another. And beyond her, now Caine could find himself in danger, too. "Oh. Of course."

"Does it make you uncomfortable to have a gun in your house?" he asked, stepping into a pair of well-worn black boots.

Emma hugged herself and gave a little shrug. "I mean, I don't love it. But I understand it. And it's not like you're asking me to shoot it."

His gaze cut toward her. "You should probably know how."

This was the strangest Christmas Day conversation ever. "I've fired guns before. I dated a Marine in college, and he was kind of a gun nut. We only lasted two months, but we went to his gun club a few times and I learned the basics of shooting."

"Well. All right, then," he said, surprise plain in his voice.

"See? I'm not all sweetness and innocence." She smirked. She liked surprising him.

Caine finished tying his laces and slanted her a sexy look. "Good to know. Now, tell me what Chewy needs. Just a pit-stop in your yard? A walk around the block?"

"The yard is fine for now, but, er, depending on how deep the snow is you might have to clear him a place to go." She grimaced. "The snow shovel's in the stairwell that goes down to the basement door."

"Got it." Caine crouched near where Chewy lay upside down on the blanket. "You want to go outside with me?" The dog flopped right-side-up and spun around excitedly. "I think that's a yes," Caine said.

"Above and beyond," she said, a little moved at seeing how nice he was to her dog. That might not seem noteworthy to some people but it meant a lot to her.

"Oh, sweetness," he said, kissing her on the forehead. "Not even close."

Chapter 13

That term of endearment wouldn't stop playing over and over in Emma's ears, which meant she couldn't stop spontaneously grinning. Or maybe the giddiness was from the two orgasms and the amazing sex. Or waking up in a man's arms on Christmas morning.

Emma freshened up and put on a pair of fleece leggings and one of her favorite long sweaters. The super-soft red cashmere had been a gift from her grandmother three years ago. And even if that hadn't been true, Emma would've adored the sweater anyway for its asymmetrical hem and loose cowl neck.

In the kitchen, Emma put on some coffee while she debated breakfast. The fact that he either didn't eat breakfast or only ate an apple explained a lot about how lean he was, hard muscle over visible bone. As tall as he was, he could've probably picked up a good twenty pounds and still looked thin.

Still debating, she had another idea for Caine, and assembled a little tin of Christmas cookies for him that she slipped into the top of his gift bag.

Finally, she settled on pancakes because she could use her oversized cookie cutters to form the batter into shapes. She mixed the batter and heated the griddle pan, then gave the big snowman-shaped cutter a light dusting of non-stick cooking spray and got the first pancake underway.

Her gaze went to the clock on the stove. It was a little after eight. Definitely late enough that Alison would be awake, but maybe not late enough that they'd be done with their present-opening bonanza. Emma didn't want to disturb that, but she also needed to decide what to do about dinner. Would it be too weird to bring Caine over? Would he even want to go? Would he think Emma should leave her house at all amid everything that was going on? Heck, did he have Christmas plans of his own to get to?

Emma flipped the first pancake, smiling to see that she'd done a decent job using the cookie cutter. She adjusted the heat for the next one, another snowman.

Even more interesting was another reaction stirring inside her—part of her wanted to stay in this bubble with Caine and see where things might go between them. Well, go beyond sex. Though she was definitely open to more of that, too.

By the time she heard Caine's boots stomping against her back porch, she had a plate full of snowmen, Santa heads, snowflakes, and Christmas trees. The keys she'd given him turned in the lock, and then Caine was back, red-nosed and grim-faced.

Emma's shoulders fell. "What?"

He shook his head. "Nothing. Everything looks clear."

Chewy raced happily to his dish, where his breakfast was already waiting.

"Oh. Really?" She searched his expression.

"Really." He came and pulled her into his arms. "Smells good in here."

She smiled. "I made festive pancakes."

"Are there any other kind?" he deadpanned.

That made her laugh. "Good point. I suppose all pancakes are, on some fundamental level, at least a little festive." She handed him the stacked-high plate. "Take that to the table for me?"

He nodded and did as she asked, and she collected everything else they needed—butter, syrup, silverware, napkins.

"Mind if I grab some coffee?" he asked.

"Nope," she said with a little smile.

"You have some yet?" he asked, eyebrow arched. She shook her head. "How do you take it?"

Her smile grew, at first because he'd thought to ask. And then, because the potential for innuendo was too good to pass up. "Any way you give it."

"Keep that up and the pancakes will be ice cold by the time I'm done with you."

Emma's smile grew wider and her pulse spiked. "Two milk, two sugar," she said.

A moment later, they settled at the table together and dug into the sweet, fluffy hotcakes. She smiled to herself when he made quick work of two and took a third.

"So, I wanted to ask you if you had plans for the day," she asked. "Somewhere you need to be later?"

He shook his head. "Some of the guys get together for Christmas dinner at the clubhouse, but I don't always go."

"Why not? If they're like your family?" She took a long sip of her coffee. He'd made it perfectly.

He tilted his head and met her waiting gaze. "I guess for so many years the day reminded me of things I'd lost or would never have, and now I just shy away from it rather than face those reminders."

It was a far more brutally honest answer than she'd expected, and her heart tripped into a sprint as goosebumps raced down her neck. All she could do was nod.

"You have plans for today?" he asked as if he hadn't just shone a light on part of the wounds inside him for her.

"I'm going to text my friend and cancel them," she said, deciding in that very instant what to do about Alison's dinner. Emma wasn't to be her only guest anyway. Alison's big family numbered more than twenty when everyone came. Her bestie would understand. "I'd like to spend the day with you."

He gave a nod, though his gaze didn't quite meet hers, but she would've sworn she saw a little smile play around those full lips. "You gonna eat that last snowflake?" he asked, pointing at the nearly empty platter with his fork.

"Nope. That snowflake has your name all over it," she said, really freaking satisfied to see him enjoying what she'd made. Not that pancakes were any big deal, but it seemed like the fact that he was eating a real meal might've been.

"I bet you're a real good teacher," he said, drizzling syrup on each of the arms of the snowflake.

She pressed a hand to her chest, where an odd, warm pressure seemed to fill the space around her heart. "Why's that?"

"Because you make even the littlest things special."

"I try," she said, moved far beyond those words. The minute he finished the pancake, she grinned. "Ready for a little surprise?"

He gave her a skeptical look again. "Sure."

She laughed. "Come on, then. It's time for presents." He rose slowly, and she took him by the hand. She grabbed her laptop off the dining room table as they passed it by, and then she led him to the blanket again.

"Emma, I don't have…" He shook his head, discomfort so plain on his face it made her ache.

She kissed him and stroked her hand from his cheek into his hair. "You already gave me *you*, silly. Your time, your protection, your company. Without you, I'd be completely alone in this. So you gave me exactly what I needed."

She thought his eyes couldn't blaze at her more, and then she handed him his gift.

"What's this?" he asked, his voice near to a whisper.

She set a new chew toy in front of Chewy, and then she pulled a present in front of herself. "Our presents," she said, grinning. "Santa left one for each of us."

"Emma—"

"Trust me, it's just something little." She gestured for him to open it.

Finally, he pulled the tissue from the bag, then lifted out its contents—the tin of cookies and six-pack of bottled orange soda.

"I wanted you to have something to open," she said. "And I thought that you could take a little taste of me home with you."

His brow furrowed as he stared at the things on the floor in front of him. He swallowed thickly, and finally nodded. "Thank you," he said, finally lifting his gaze. Were his eyes glassy?

The possibility that she was really seeing what she thought she was made her heart hurt. Because none of the reasons that she could imagine for why such a hastily thrown-together present would affect him so much were good. "Okay, my turn," she said, pulling her wrapped package to her. "When my grandmother died, I started two new traditions. This one's kinda silly, but it gives me something to look forward to."

"Tell me," he said.

She smoothed her hands over the colorful paper. "Early in the year, I find something I really want, something that's kind of a splurge. And then I save money from each paycheck until I can afford it. Then I wrap it up and give it to myself for Christmas."

He looked at her like she was maybe a little crazy. "What did you get?"

Grinning, she pressed the metallic green bow to the side of her hair and then tore open the paper, shreds going everywhere, until finally her new baby was revealed before her. "A new MacBook. Fifteen-inch screen. With all the bells and whistles. My current laptop is more than three years old and freezes up all the time." She hugged the box awkwardly to her chest. "I've been waiting for this for so long." She laughed. But at twenty-five hundred dollars, it was a big deal to have finally gotten this for herself. "I know, I'm a huge dork."

Just watching her, Caine shook his head.

"I have one more present to give. Want to help me?" she asked, setting up her old laptop atop the box for her new one.

"How could I help?"

Her fingers moved over the keyboard as she pulled up the three websites. "I put away part of every paycheck throughout the year so that I can make a Christmas Day donation to a local charity. I usually try to pick something that has to do with kids, but it's so hard to choose. What do you think?"

She clicked through the three sites, and Caine leaned in to view them with her. One foundation worked to help children of working-class families that made too much for government assistance but too little to fully provide for their kids. Emma saw this with many of her children at school, kids whose families didn't have enough money for school supplies or new backpacks or even new shoes to fit growing feet. The second organization was a center and shelter dedicated to helping LGBTQ homeless youths, who were disproportionately likely to face homelessness and, once they ended up on the street, experienced greater levels of violence than other youths. And the third organization was the county's CASA program, which assigned court-appointed special advocates for abused and neglected children who otherwise might be lost in the over-burdened child welfare system. Emma had worked with a few volunteers from this program over the years, and knew they did good work.

"I have a little over three thousand dollars saved," she said, turning to him. "What do you—"

His eyes were brimming with unshed tears. And his effort to

restrain them highlighted every sharp angle on his face.

"Caine?"

"Don't," he rasped, his eyelids closing like he was in pain. A single tear streaked from the corner of one eye.

"I'm going to hug you," she whispered.

"Emma," he said, his voice like it'd been scoured with sandpaper. He dropped his head into his hands.

Slowly, she crawled so that she knelt behind him. She came in close, her thighs around his hips, her arms around his stomach, her head laying on his broad back. She felt the hard outline of the holstered gun against her belly, but she didn't care. "I'm here now, Caine. Okay?"

He didn't answer for a long time. And she wasn't surprised, given how hard he worked to rein in the emotion trying to break free. She felt his effort in the clenching of his stomach muscles, in the shudders wracking through his back, in the unevenness of his breathing. In the end, Emma wasn't at all sure whether it was better that he'd fought it back, or if it would've been better if he'd let it out. Whatever *it* was.

Finally, he threaded his fingers through hers against his chest. "Do you still want my opinion?" he asked, his voice raw.

She stroked the back of his hair, noticing up close for the first time that black tattoos filled in the two most noticeable places near his hairline where scars kept his hair from growing. "Absolutely."

"They're all kids, so of course they're all worthy. The Ravens work with CASA a lot so I know they're good people. But, the LGBTQ homeless shelter. That would be my vote."

It was personal to him, that much was clear. And that was all she needed to know. "That's who we'll give to, then."

"We?"

"Yes, Caine. We."

He heaved a breath. "Don't you want to know why?"

"Very much," she said, because she wanted to know everything about this man. "But only if you want to tell me."

He didn't respond. There were only so many reasons an organization like that might mean so much to him. Either someone he cared about could've benefitted from the services they offered and maybe hadn't had the opportunity. Or *he* could've benefitted from their services himself. And if that was true, did that mean he was bi? Or another identity altogether?

She reached out, tugged her laptop closer, and pecked all her information into the donation form with one hand while she continued embracing him with the other. "The fun part is hitting the *Submit* button. That's all you."

He peered over his shoulder at her, like he was trying to see if she was for real. She nodded, and he clicked the button. The confirmation page came up with a row of kids' beautiful smiling faces.

"You give good presents, Emma Kerry," he finally said. How was it that he thought he wasn't sweet again?

She smiled where she leaned against his back. "I just like trying to make people happy."

"What other traditions do you have?" he asked, turning toward her.

"Christmas movie marathon with copious amounts of cookies and chocolate-drizzled popcorn as snacks."

He peered up, and *Jesus* he was so freaking gorgeous to her. "Got any funny Christmas movies?"

She grinned. "So many funny ones. Just you wait and see."

And if that's what it took to make Caine happy, it was only the beginning of what she would do.

Chapter 14

Caine couldn't remember ever laughing so much. At the movies themselves, which ranged from funny to stupid to *terrible*. At how much the movies made Emma laugh. At how passionate she was in defending their humorous qualities.

All day, she'd kept things light and playful between them as they laid on a big makeshift bed of blankets and pillows on her living room floor. They'd never stopped touching and kissing, some part of their bodies always tangled up in the other. He'd been half hard for hours but hadn't acted on it because this kind of closeness wasn't something he'd ever had before, either.

To say nothing of how much he'd eaten.

Emma had just filled him up, heart, mind, and fucking soul.

And after the way he'd almost shattered this morning, he'd needed every bit of her lightness. Between the connection and the sex and the gift, he'd already been overwhelmed. And then she'd shared her tradition of giving to charities. All charities for kids in need. It made sense, of course. She was a kindergarten teacher. But then she'd pulled up that website for the LGBTQ shelter and it'd been one emotional brick more than his badly crumbling inner walls could support.

He'd looked for places like that when he'd gone on the run as a fourteen-year-old. And again before he'd found ways to use his body for food and shelter as a fifteen-year-old. And again when a pimp had tried—and failed—to pressure him with intimidation and ply him with drugs to work for him as a seventeen-year-old. But places like that shelter hadn't existed fifteen years ago, at least not where he'd grown up in small-town Ohio. And once the wrong people knew you'd shown interest in someone of the same sex, or even if there were just rumors, they'd make sure your life was a living hell if you showed up at the shelters that did exist. Beds were scarce, after all, and not everyone who wanted one got one. They made sure you learned not to even show up. So Caine had run and hitched and done whatever he needed to survive.

"What are you thinking about so hard?" Emma asked, tilting her head against his shoulder to peer up at him.

He was so relaxed—for once—that he was able to just let himself talk. "Your present was the first one I ever got that was meant just for me," he said, knowing he wasn't explaining himself well. "When I was a kid in the group home, the house parents got all of us the same exact thing—one year, it was a package of socks, a Pez dispenser with a couple packets of those little rectangular candies, and a new flannel shirt for the boys. And if someplace like a church sent a donation, we'd all get the same stuffed animal or the same set of dominos or the same deck of cards." He twisted a length of blond around his fingers, still blown away that he could just touch her like this. "You actually thought of our time together and came up with a gift that you knew would mean something to me, personally."

She burrowed in tighter against him. "Can I ask why you lived in a home?"

Caine sighed. "You can ask me anything, Emma. I mean that. I'm just warning you that I'm gonna suck at answering. And shit's gonna catch me off guard like…like it did this morning."

"I want to know you, Caine, however you are." She threaded her fingers between his and pulled his hand to her mouth for a kiss.

"How are you so fucking perfect?" The question spilled out of his mouth, but in truth it'd been playing on a loop in his head for *hours*.

"I'm not perfect, Caine. And I think you need to take me off of the pedestal I fear you're putting me on. I haven't done a great job of building any kind of community around myself since my grandmother died three years ago, and I'm lonely a lot. I have two really good girlfriends, but they're both married, and one has a young son. There's only so much I can lean on them." She kissed his knuckles again. "I started a graduate degree in teaching four years ago that I haven't finished because all those evening classes were part of the reason why I didn't realize my grandmother was as sick as she was. And I could've been spending those hours with her. After she died, I couldn't force myself to go back, so it's like I doubly wasted that time, because in the end I didn't have her or the degree. So I'm not perfect. As best I can figure, we're all just trying."

The words sank into his skin, as if they were looking for places they might stay within him forever. He wished they would. "Fair enough," he said. "My mother died of a heroin overdose and my father decided taking care of a five-year-old was a pain in the ass. So I ended up in the system."

Sadness hung on her pretty features, and he hated that he'd put it there. "Same age as my kids," she said. "That breaks my heart. No wonder you're so strong."

Stunned, he shook his head. Half the time he felt entirely out of control. Half the time he threw up walls out of fear. And half the time he opted out of life before anyone had the chance to discard him. No matter that the math didn't add up, it was just how he felt. "Eventually, I fell in with a man who wasn't just willing to give me a job, but also to teach me and take me in. Jerry Tiller. I wouldn't be whatever I am today without him." Of course, he'd just skipped over all the most crucial years, but he couldn't...not yet...

She searched his face, and her expression was so open to everything he was telling her. But she still didn't know the worst of him, and all these hours of falling were going to hurt like hell when he woke up face-down on the concrete.

In the meantime, she kept surprising him. "And was Jerry your boyfriend?"

He blinked. Well. Okay, then. He supposed he should've expected that given the way he'd reacted to helping that shelter, except very few people he'd ever met were willing to confront the truth the way Emma did. And always in a way that made it safe to give that honesty right back.

"No," he said, pressing a kiss against Emma's soft hair. His heart suddenly hammered, because his next words weren't ones he usually voiced. Or, like, *ever*. "I've been with men, Em, but I've never had a boyfriend. Mostly, I was just..." He shook his head, struggling to figure out how to explain his bisexuality to someone else for the first time. Hell, to explain it to himself, too. "My whole life, I've just looked for connection wherever I could find it. Does that...does that bother you?"

She brought her face closer to his, and Caine nearly held his breath.

"I've had lovers before you, Caine. Does that bother you?"

He frowned. "The idea of someone else touching you right *now* makes me want to smash things with my head, but I don't resent that you had a life before."

"Then why would I resent the same for you?" she asked, expression totally sincere.

Could she really be so okay with this? He gave a bewildered little shrug. "I don't know," he said in a low voice. Then, stronger, "Jerry wasn't a boyfriend. He was the first adult in my whole life who actually took care of me. No strings attached. I bought my first bike with money I earned at his shop, and when he died and his son sold off the business, I hit the road on my own and found the Ravens. That was a decade ago."

With every new thing he shared, he felt like a thin filament stretched between them, anchoring them together. The connection between them was growing, strengthening. He could *feel* it like he'd never felt anything before.

Caine was getting *attached*. To that feeling. To Emma herself.

It was what he'd *always* wanted. It was the thing he feared the most.

But right now, he had it. He had her. And he wanted her…

"Stand up, Emma." The questions in her gaze quickly shifted to understanding, and she rose above him. His hands went to her waistband and quickly bared her. Caine pulled her until she stood with her feet on either side of him where he sat leaning against the front of the couch. "I want my mouth on you again."

The moan that spilled out of her at the first swipe of his tongue went right to his cock. He unzipped his jeans and shoved them down his thighs. Then he held her open with his thumbs so that her clit was right where he wanted it to be. He sucked and flicked and nipped until she was thrusting against his face. He groaned his approval. Her hips became more frantic. "*Caine*," she cried hoarsely, her knees going out such that she nearly collapsed into his lap, still shaking.

He took advantage and kissed her, wanting some part of him inside of her while her orgasm wrung every second of pleasure out of her.

"Jesus, your mouth should be illegal," she said, chuffing out a breathless laugh.

"You say the nicest things," he said, the playful words probably masking just how much he lapped up her praise. "Will you take me in you?"

She didn't hesitate—she shifted to her knees. They both shucked their shirts. He pulled his last condom from his wallet and rolled it on.

She impaled herself on him, inch by soul-stealing inch. "You fill me up so good," she said.

The echo of his earlier thought stretched a new filament of connection between them. "Ride me, Emma. Show me how you like it."

Her fingers dug into his shoulders and she shifted so that she crouched on her feet instead of kneeling, allowing her to bounce faster, harder, deeper.

She pressed their faces together, her pants ghosting over his skin. "The way you took me this morning, Caine, that's how I've always wanted it. But I'd never been able to find it before. That intensity is all you."

Sensation squeezed his balls. "You telling me you like it rough, Em?"

"Yes," she cried, her thrusts taking on a more frantic edge again.

"Fuck," he gritted out. Grasping her hips, he forced her down harder.

She unleashed a high-pitched moan and tossed her head back, giving him a beautiful, orgasm-inducing view of her breasts bouncing with every thrust.

"How rough?" he asked, reaching between them to squeeze the base of his cock—hard. Just voicing the question had given him a shove toward the edge.

Those summery blues were so filled with arousal, and like the greedy motherfucker he was, he wanted more of it. "I don't know. But I want to find out."

He wound a sudden tight fist into her hair and dragged her against him, then tugged on her to slam her down on his cock. "Like this?"

The moan was its own answer, but still he loved hearing "*Yes.*"

He wrapped his other hand around the base of her throat and squeezed enough to apply pressure but no more, but the real beauty was the way his two-handed leverage allowed him not just to slam her down but to thrust up. "*This?*"

Her eyes rolled back in her head and her mouth dropped open. "Caine," she rasped. "Don't stop."

"Not a chance," he said, memorizing what she looked like moving above him, giving herself over to him. "You're going to take me just like this, aren't you?"

"Please."

"Yeah."

"How about this?" he asked, releasing her throat and landing a smack against her ass. Then another.

"Oh, *God*," she moaned, falling against him so that her front was tight to his.

"Somebody likes having her ass played with, does she?" he asked, remembering the way his touch against her rear opening had beckoned her orgasm. "You can tell me."

"I do. I like it," she babbled, her hips frantic again. She ground herself against him, her clit rocking against the muscle of his lower belly.

"Get me really wet." He held two fingers to her mouth. "Suck."

On a moan, she bathed his fingers with her tongue and took his fingertips to the back of her throat. "Yes, sweet girl, that's right. Nice and wet for your asshole."

"Caine," she groaned as he pulled her hair to still her and hold her tight against him, opening her rear for his touch.

He swirled his wet fingertips against the tight opening, and that by itself made her whole body jerk against him. "So fucking sensitive, Emma. Anybody ever taken you here?"

A quick shake of her head. "*Nooo*." The reply was a moan as he slowly slipped his middle finger in to the first knuckle, then the second. "Oh God."

The finger fucking he gave her was gentle—until she started working herself back against his penetration. "Wanna try two?"

Her forehead rested against his. "Anything. Everything."

Jesus, this woman. He reached to her core where he was still deep inside her and swiped at more slick wetness. He stacked his fingertips, narrowing the invasion, letting her get used to it before he was finally finger-fucking her again. And she was right there with him, trying to move with his movements. He released her hair. "Fuck both my fingers and my cock, Emma. Ride me 'til you come."

Her nails dug into his shoulders then, and she was absolutely uninhibited as she ground and slammed against him. He clenched his jaw so hard that his teeth hurt, but he didn't want to shoot before she got there. It was just that his fingers made her even tighter, and her cum was already spilling out onto his balls, and her sounds were like the dirtiest fucking soundtrack he'd ever heard.

Suddenly she was gasping for breath, then holding it, then screaming his name as she jerked against him, her whole body spasming, her orgasm nearly pushing his cock out of her. And then he couldn't hold back another second. He eased his fingers out and cradled her as he took her down to the ground beneath him, and then he went at her like he was trying to crawl inside her and never come out.

His orgasm roared down his spine and nailed him in the ass, shoving him deep as his cock kicked again and again. He was panting and sweaty, and so was she, but he'd never seen anyone more beautiful than Emma Kerry in that moment—laying beneath him, thoroughly fucked, hair a sexed-up mess, lips swollen and red, eyes glazed over with the sexual satisfaction he'd given her.

"That was amazing, Caine," she said. "Yes to all that."

She was entirely serious, but the deadpan delivery still made him grin.

Then she chuckled.

And Chewy eyeballed and sniffed them because they were on the floor. Again. Caine laughed as hard as Emma did.

Which was the moment Caine first questioned if the intense pressure inside his chest could be love.

* * * *

Caine spent that night. Then the next night and the night after that. Until nearly a week had passed and so, along with it, had all but the last day of the old year.

Emma only had today and tomorrow left in her winter break, and then classes would resume and she and Caine would have to leave the secluded retreat they'd built around themselves.

She'd put off her friends, promising Alison that she'd finally tell her everything that was going on, and he'd put off his brothers in the club unless it was something that might offer the slightest clue about her stalker.

Though the sheriff was interviewing the handful of people she could remotely think of, there was only one really good lead, in Caine's opinion. And that had apparently come from some ex-military friend in

Baltimore who was a computer genius willing to bend a few rules to hack into traffic cameras. Particularly, one camera which offered a view of the street down which you had to exit when pulling out of the elementary school driveway. Apparently, he'd assumed that the vandalism had occurred at night, and following that thinking, he'd scanned that camera's feed during the overnight hours each day of the weekend when the damage occurred.

That had produced a list of seventeen vehicles. It seemed like a lot to narrow down to Emma, but Caine had thought it was their first big break. Now all they could do was wait.

It was wearing on Caine.

Especially since nothing else had happened around her house. Or if it had, they had fewer ways to tell. By Thursday, the temperatures had rebounded into the low fifties, and by Friday all but the bigger snow piles had melted.

So their retreat was nearly over, school was about to begin, and—

"We're no fucking closer to identifying this asshole than we were a week ago," Caine grumbled as he paced in her small kitchen and scrubbed at his hair.

He had a habit of doing that when he got worked up about something, and it gave him a look like he'd just rolled out of bed after having sex with her. And that pretty much made Emma want to drag him back to bed to make that come true.

Because, good God, Caine was giving her the best sex of her life. On the floor, the couch, her bed (of course), and on the steps when they hadn't been able to make it up to her bed. In the shower and bent over the kitchen counter. For six days they hadn't held back once from indulging in each other. And even though she was exhausted and sore, Emma didn't want it to end.

Not ever.

Not ever. Her heart panged. Because apparently, it only took six days of non-stop sex with the man willing to risk himself to protect her to make Emma fall in love.

"We will be when your friend finishes his analysis of the traffic camera, though, right?"

He growled and stalked out of the kitchen. Each of the past two days, Caine's frustration had grown. And since she knew it was born of misplaced guilt and concern for her, she didn't hold it against him. In truth, she was frustrated, too. Because she had no idea how she was supposed to go about her normal routine knowing she had a stalker.

"What should I make for breakfast?" she called.

"Whatever you want. I'm not hungry," came his reply.

She stepped into the doorway that led to the dining room and found him peering out the front windows. Grinning, she shimmied her panties down and stepped out of them, leaving herself naked beneath her long sleepshirt. "How about me for breakfast then?"

When he peered at her, she twirled the lacey scrap of fabric on her finger and gave him her best sexy look.

His expression softened. "You're too fucking sexy for your own good."

She made her way to the living room. "Right back at you, biker man." She gave him a pointed once over in that Under Armour shirt. Never intending to stay the night, let alone a week, he'd been in the same outfit, alternating between wearing the black long-sleeve and the white short-sleeve and washing the lot of it every other day. But as far as she was concerned, he could wear that black base layer for the rest of his life and she'd never get tired of seeing the way it clung to the shape of him.

Suddenly, he came at her. "Have you thought about what that really means yet?" he asked, his voice harsher than she'd heard in more than a week.

"What?" she asked, bewildered.

"That I'm a biker. A Raven Rider. And that sometimes we cross lines when we have to." He nailed her with a stare.

"Uh, okay. I mean, your friend is illegally hacking into a government camera system. For me. So how judgmental can I be about—"

"I got shot," he said, cutting her off as he held up his hand, the one with all the scars stretching down over the wrist. She'd asked about it one day, but it was one of those questions he hadn't answered. "A lowlife from a gang in Baltimore drove by Dare's house and shot it up while a bunch of us were there. Haven and her friend, Cora, were both shot, too, and ended up in surgery fighting for their lives. One of my brother's little boys, too."

She gasped. "Oh, my God."

"Ask me what happened to the shooter." He arched a brow over eyes so suddenly cold that she could hardly meet his gaze.

"Why are you do—"

"*Ask* me," he said, getting up in her space.

"Stop it," she said, not because she didn't want to know, but because what he was doing here wasn't informational.

"We don't hide from the truth, right, Em?" The hint of a mocking tone was more than she could take.

"Right, which is why I have to say that you're being a dick." Now she was the one arching a brow. "You have things you want to talk about, Caine. I'm always happy to talk or to listen. But don't you dare do this."

Something flashed behind his eyes. Regret? Fear? Resolve? She wasn't sure, because then it was gone again and this…meanness was back. "I'll tell you what happened to him. A couple of us went after him and the guy who told him where we were, and we caught them. And then, knowing that one man had repeatedly done things to hurt and endanger our members, and the other had just shot four of our people and would just keep coming for us if we let him go—"

"Caine, stop. Stop!" Emma yelled, already knowing what he was going to say.

But he said it anyway. "—we killed them both."

"Oh," she moaned, her head spinning. Or maybe the floor was tilting. She wasn't sure. She wasn't sure of anything anymore. Not when the man she loved was revealing his past to her as if it were a weapon and landing such shocking blows.

"That's not all you ought to know about me, though," he said, his voice sounding like it came from a stranger. "Hell, no, there's more."

Emma pressed her hands to her ears. She knew it was childish, but she could hardly breathe for the massive weight sitting on her chest. She needed time to process. To calm down. For *him* to calm down.

It didn't stop him and he didn't calm. "Let's see, I've taken money, food, and shelter before in exchange for sex. But, I mean, it can't surprise you that much that I'm a dirty slut given the way I fuck. And most of the time these days I only fuck strangers, even couples, I meet online. Until you."

Why was he taking the amazing connection they'd shared and trying to twist it into an ugly thing? Her stomach rolled. She refused to bite, just absolutely refused to allow him to make her question it, too. Even though, damn him, the pain just left of center in her chest proved that his barbs were hitting true.

"You're *trying* to hurt me, Caine McKannon. You're trying to hurt *us*. And I'm not going to stand here and take it." She made for the steps.

He grasped her by the arm and hauled her back against his chest. "I'm just coming clean with you, Em. Finally. And you have to hear this one more gem about me. It's the best one yet, I promise."

"Let me go," she rasped, losing against the sting of threatening tears. She really didn't want to cry in front of him.

"It's about a sweet, innocent little angel named Grace. Just six years old. Same as your kids. Looked up to me like I could protect her from *anything*." His voice cracked, and her brain latched onto that one little show of an emotion other than rage. Latched onto it *hard* even though it probably meant nothing.

But she turned, and the shift made them both stumble until he was pinning her against the wall at the foot of the stairs. "How old are you in this story?" she managed.

He ignored her. "Except, as sweet, innocent angels do, she misjudged me. Believed in me when she shouldn't have. And then there was a fire."

Oh, God. She couldn't believe *this* was how she was going to find out what he'd been through. "How old, Caine?" she asked again, the first tear falling.

"House parents both smoked in bed. One lost his life to it." He shrugged. "Deserved it, too. But he wasn't the only one. You see, the flames engulfed that whole side of the connected duplex where the girls' room was. And Grace, she hadn't escaped because she was hiding a cat in her closet. A cat I knew about and helped her hide."

Grace...oh, *Grace*. The tattoo on his chest. The pressure from the tears that needed to fall almost choked her, but still she asked, "How old?"

He shook her. "That *doesn't* matter. All that matters is that I told her I'd save her, but the flames blocked the stairs. And the only other way out was the fire escape that had been broken for a long time because our so-called fucking caregivers were abusive cheapskates who only spent money when social services was coming for an evaluation. It took me forever to convince Grace to climb out because she refused to leave the cat behind, but finally the stray crawled out the window on its own. By then the room was filling with smoke and flames. The fire moved so fast. *So fast*, Em. We couldn't breathe. I picked her up and made her hold on tight to my neck, and then I climbed out the window. I knew where to step. Where the old iron was weak and where it was solid."

He gasped in a breath, and the words turned into a scary, hollow monotone that broke Emma's heart more than anything else she'd heard.

"T-there was this weird moan from inside the house, and then suddenly fire shot out through the windows. My shirt and hair caught fire. Grace screamed that her arm and leg..." He choked on the words. "I misstepped." The sound that came out of him was unlike anything she'd ever heard from another human. "The grating gave way. We...we fell. Two stories. I was supposed to protect her. I told her I would. She...she l-landed under me. B-beautiful little Grace..."

Emma threw her arms around him, her face wet with tears she could no longer fight. "Listen to me, there's no age at which that would've been your fault, Caine. Someone else's carelessness set the fire. Someone else's negligence failed to fix the fire escape."

A fast shake of his head as he pulled free of her embrace. "You don't understand."

She wouldn't let him loose. "I do. You loved Grace."

"It should've been me. That's what the other monster said when she came to my hospital room. It should've been me."

Pain lanced through Emma's chest. "What a horrible, unforgiveable thing to say. You were a child," she said, putting the truth out there whether he wanted to admit it or not.

He pounded his fist into the wall beside her. "I should've saved her! I gave my word!"

Emma flinched, but she wasn't giving up. "You tried—"

"Stop it!" he yelled, his voice breaking. "How can you even stand me?"

She bit back a sob. "Were you fifteen? Fourteen? Thirteen?"

"I told you it doesn't fucking matter," he rasped, his voice hoarse and shattered, his face a twisted mask of horror and grief.

"Were you twelve, Caine?" He shook his head, those pale eyes so, so bleak. "Eleven?" she said, her belly in utter knots. "Ten?" came out at a whisper.

"Stop," he cried, nearly collapsing against her. "*I'm sorry.*"

Oh, God. *Oh, God. Ten!*

His hands fisted in her shirt. "*I'm so sorry.*"

They went limp and slid down the wall in a pile of sweaty bodies and tangled limbs. If Emma felt gutted and empty and raw, she could only imagine what Caine felt. A shudder wracked through his whole body.

"It's okay," she rasped. "It's okay." She pulled his head against her chest and stroked his hair, whispering those words again and again, like someone should've done for him twenty damn years ago. Her stomach hurt so bad she feared she'd throw up, and a headache bloomed behind her eyes. None of which compared to his pain. Pain he'd shouldered nearly his whole life.

He'd warned her. He'd warned her he wasn't normal and that there were big things she didn't know. Of course, she didn't hold Grace's death against him. He'd tried to save her. What'd happened to the both of them had been a tragedy. And no way would she ever criticize him for the things that had kept him alive long enough to find her.

She swallowed hard.

But the shooting…

A chill crawled over her skin.

She didn't know what to make of that. And certainly not with the way her head spun and throbbed.

Of course that was the moment Caine's cell phone rang. He made no move to answer it, and after four rings, the tone cut off.

Then started again.

Stopped, then started again.

"Could be important," Emma whispered, trying to fish it from his jeans pocket.

"I-I got it," he said, his hands so gentle as he took it from her. He accepted the call and pressed it to his ear. "What do you want, Dare? This isn't a good time."

Chapter 15

"Fuck," Caine said, disconnecting the call. "We're getting intel back this afternoon from the traffic camera. Dare asked us to come over before the New Year's Eve dinner gets underway so that the whole Ravens' board could hear what's going on."

Not that Caine was going to that dinner, or the party after. Hell, Caine would be lucky to be able to stomach food for a good week after this...this absolute *blood-letting*.

His and that of the only woman he'd ever loved.

No doubt she wouldn't want to go either. Or be anywhere near him.

"Okay," she said, rising onto shaky legs. And Christ if she wasn't still naked beneath that shirt from when she'd tried to turn his shit mood around by seducing him.

For two days now, panic and anxiety had snowballed inside him until he couldn't breathe, couldn't sleep, couldn't eat. Until he'd convinced himself that he'd already failed again, that Emma was already dead and they just didn't know it yet. No matter what he said or what he did, it wasn't going to matter when the outcome was so predetermined. At least, that's what the anxiety told him. Or maybe it was the PTSD? Who the hell knew which part of his brain told him the lies that always sounded more convincing than the truth?

He grabbed Emma's hand. "I'm sorry," he rasped, knowing he'd destroyed this with his own two hands but still owing her that much.

"Me, too," she said, giving his hand a gentle squeeze before letting go. "I'll get dressed quick."

Chewy stood at the bottom of the steps and looked back and forth between where Caine still sat and Emma now went. Back and forth, back and forth.

"You should go to her," Caine said. "She might need you."

Chewy climbed up on Caine's thigh with his little front paws, tilted his head, and gave a little whine.

"I don't deserve you, little man. Go get her. Go on, now."

The dog got the message and did his funny little hop-run up the steps. Then Caine finally scraped himself up off the floor. Gathered his things. Tugged his skull cap into place. Holstered his gun at the small of his back. And waited by the door with his winter riding gear in his hand.

He wasn't sure how he was standing. For twenty-one years, the weight of that story had filled him. And now that he'd let it out, he didn't even have that unspoken shame to hold him up. He'd never been emptier than he was right that second.

True to her word, Emma descended five minutes later wearing a pair of tall leather boots over skinny jeans, a pale yellow sweater, and her hair in a chunky braid that hung down one side. No make-up. Puffy eyes she hadn't tried to hide.

She was so fucking perfect... No, she was *someone else's* fucking perfect now. Someone who actually deserved her.

"I'm parked out back," he said.

"I'm just down the street," she said.

He frowned. "I'm not sure we should ride apart."

She shrugged. "I don't see the point in riding together. You'll just have to bring me back again. And I assumed, I don't know..." She shrugged again, and the defeated blankness was like a steel knife to his windpipe.

His mind churned. Caine needed someone keeping 24/7 watch, but it didn't have to be him, not if it made her uncomfortable. "Okay, we'll take your car."

"Bye, ChewChew," she said, voice so devastatingly flat. She swiped at the whole panel of light switches on the living room wall. The Christmas tree went dark.

It was the first time he'd seen it off the entire time he'd been there. Hell, even before she'd invited him to stay on Christmas Eve, that tree had been lit every other time he'd been by or watched over her house.

The darkness was so fucking wrong that he wanted to rage at the world. But he'd already done that, hadn't he? That was how they'd gotten here in the first place.

Walking side by side outside, they were miles apart.

"Damnit," Emma said, cutting into the street near her car. "This will take forever to clear." The plows had used the empty space in front of Emma's little CRV to pile snow, resulting in the whole front and front side of her car being behind a wall of snow, not to mention the three-foot-high wall that separated the car from the street. "Your bike it is, I guess."

He gave her clothing a once-over.

"What?" Her gaze dared him to give her a hard time.

He shook his head. "It's a good outfit for riding. That's all."

They cut through the alley to the little nook along her back fence where he'd left his motorcycle for the past week. Better than out on the street getting knocked over by a plow or sprayed with salt. If Emma's situation hadn't felt so dire with having found the broken window and footprints, he would've eventually gone home and traded out his Harley for the old pick-up he owned. Because riding in storm conditions like last weekend was fucking stupid. But now the roads and weather were clear again, so they should be fine to get to the compound.

He removed and stowed the cover, checked that the cold hadn't too badly fucked with the tire pressure, and handed Emma the helmet and coat. "Put this on. Riding gear, too."

She accepted the helmet. "What about you?"

"I've ridden without a helmet a million times. It's only fifteen minutes."

She frowned. "That's not smart."

He chuffed out a laugh. "You're right," he said as he made sure the helmet's fit was snug.

"Why do I need the Stormtrooper coat, too?"

He shouldn't have found her face so cute through the helmet's visor, but he did. Cute and sexy. Before he'd messed everything up, he would've teased her about the coat's nickname. But he no longer had to ask the why of it, since they'd watched six of the Star Wars movies together over the course of the week. He got the reference.

"You'll be too cold without it," he said. *And if I fuck anything else up today, it'll keep you safe.* But he didn't add that because she didn't need to shoulder anymore bullshit from him. And he was a good fucking rider, so that was the one area he never had to doubt himself.

"So then you'll be cold?" she asked.

How could she even care at this point? After he'd wielded his dirtiest secrets against her like a blade. "I've got layers and Cold Gear on. I'll be fine. Now, I'm about to throw a shit-ton of information at you. Tell me to slow down if you need to." In ten minutes, he gave her a crash-course in being a motorcycle passenger. How to get on and off, where to hold him, where to put her feet, what to expect for different actions and movements on the bike. "Our communication will be limited, so tap me once on the right shoulder for *stop when it's convenient* and twice on the right for *stop right now*. If you want to tell me you have a problem, tap me once on the left shoulder, or if you need me to slow down, tap the left twice. That should cover it for a ride this short. And I'll take it easy."

"I think I got it," she said, her face full of concentration.

On a long sigh, Caine mounted his bike and gave her a nod when he was ready for her. It was another first for him, sharing his bike with the woman he loved. It should've been special. It should've rocked his fucking world. And it did, but only because it meant none of the things it should've meant.

"This okay?" she said, when she settled in tightly behind him. He didn't exactly own a bike ideally equipped for a passenger's comfort, so she was doing better than okay.

"Yes," he said, pulling her arms around him more firmly and ignoring the fuck outta how good this should've felt. Did *still* feel. He slid on his sunglasses. "Just remember, Emma, no matter what, hold on tight."

* * * *

This would've been super cool and exciting if being wrapped around Caine wasn't pure torture. He didn't want her touching him, she knew that. And she wasn't sure what she thought of him either. All of this was just for expediency. And hopefully the Ravens would find something that would bring this whole thing to an end and put them both out of their misery.

Because those few minutes away from him as she'd dressed had made it easier to breathe, easier to think, easier to realize that Caine had apparently revisited that argument about whether they should be together. And *no* had won, judging by the way he'd tried so hard to push her away.

So, who was she kidding? She was already so head over heels that misery was in her future either way. Yay her.

"Okay, here we go. Nice and easy," he said.

Emma clutched him and concentrated on keeping her body neutral and letting it lean how he wanted it to lean. So far that was no problem at all. True to his word, he turned into the alley gently, went slow, and pulled out into traffic on the street just as smooth as glass. He kept a good distance from the cars around him and braked with room to spare. At the third light, the bike came to a rougher stop.

He turned his head to call back to her. "Brakes are acting a little funny. Probably from a week of sitting out in that weather. I'll take it slow. Just wanted to alert you that we might stop a little rough like that. I got it."

"Okay," she said, appreciating the communication.

When the light turned green, Emma clung tight. But Caine was right, the stops were jerky. Toward the edge of town, they rolled to a stop at a light, but mostly halted moving because he'd used his boots on the ground. Luckily, they'd been the only vehicle at this side of the intersection so it hadn't been any problem.

A car rolled up next to them as Caine turned his head to talk over his left shoulder. "I think I'm gonna have to— *Fuck,* Em! Hold on!"

The Harley took off on a hard throttle, shooting them forward and forcing Emma to use every bit of the strength in her arms and thighs to stay in her seat.

She wanted to ask him what he'd seen and what was wrong, but there was only one explanation for why he was now barreling out Route 15, weaving in and out of cars, and running yellow lights.

Yellow lights that another vehicle ran, too, judging by the revving engine she heard.

She tried to peer over her shoulder to see what was coming up behind them, but Caine gripped her hands, hard. A silent command to be steady. A silent reminder that he was there. And they were in this together.

Caine ran another yellow light. Their speed climbed. The car pursued. How were they going to stop from going this fast when they'd been struggling at twenty-five and thirty miles an hour?

His hand held something up to her. In her panic, it took her eyes a moment to focus. But then she saw. It was his cell, and he'd dialed *9-1-1*.

Oh, God, help us. She patted his stomach in acknowledgement and he pocketed the phone, and then he reached his hand between them, underneath his sweatshirt, and pulled his gun from its holster. The wind carried away Emma's cry.

Suddenly, he was gripping her wrist hard, and it made her grip him harder, too. Maybe that's what he intended, because the next thing Emma knew, Caine pulled a fast right-hand turn that tilted them terrifyingly low to the ground. With his left hand, he fired past her. *One, two, three* shots.

Squealing tires were the only thing Emma knew for sure, other than that the bike blessedly returned upright again—and was still going really, really fucking fast. Away from Route 15, the road quickly turned more residential, then more rural, and he allowed them to coast so that the bike lost speed naturally. As they slowed, her heart finally slipped down from her throat, where it'd been attempting an escape from her body.

And she wasn't the only one, because Caine's heart beat hard and fast enough that she felt it where her hands still clutched at him.

The distant roaring revs of an engine…

The sound sent her heart right back into her throat. She knocked her helmet once into Caine's left shoulder, but he'd apparently already heard, because he went hard on the throttle, and they started regaining speed.

Anger erupted inside her right alongside the fear. Who *was* this? And what had she ever done to upset someone enough to chase her, to want to hurt her? Why in the world would someone endanger lives to get at her? She didn't understand a single bit of this. The only thing she understood was that she wanted her and Caine to survive it. And to have a chance for something after they did.

She clutched him as they took a curve in the rural road hard and tight, that terrifying dip happening again. He fired more shots, but she didn't hear tire squeals like she had last time. Suddenly, he tapped the gun against her left thigh. No, he was working into the pocket of his riding gear that hung there.

Why was he giving it to her? But she couldn't ask and, anyway, they didn't have time for even a single one of the questions she had. Instead, he pointed ahead of them. Emma looked over his shoulder. The road turned at more than a ninety-degree angle around a field of dead, golden grass. How were they going to make that turn?

He let off the throttle entirely, and then she knew. They weren't.

What did that mean? Could the motorcycle drive into the field? And if not, what were the alternatives? And, oh God, why had she allowed Caine to give her all his protective gear?

All these thoughts and more raced through her mind in mere seconds, all the time that elapsed between his pointing and their way-too-fast approach to the sharp curve. Emma held him tighter, her gaze trained on what they were hurtling towards, which was when she saw two things that made her blood run cold—the mounds of hard snow the plow had left along the edge of the road and the deep ditch that ran along the edge of the field behind those snow piles.

Caine made a gesture with his hand, as if it were an upright blade that spun and flattened. And she knew exactly what was about to happen.

She just couldn't *believe* it was about to happen.

Maybe a hundred feet. Half that. Thirty. The bike began to turn and skid. Twenty. The angle lowered and lowered, bringing them closer to the ground. Ten. Emma could see the specks of rocks in the snow now.

She expected the weight of the bike to crush her leg, but for a long second, it felt like she was flying on Caine's back. Somewhere near her, metal and plastic screeched against asphalt. And then she collided with the ground in a cold cushioning crunch. She lost Caine upon impact, and then her body was rolling over rough, uneven ground until she came to a hard stop at the bottom of that wet, weedy ditch.

I'm alive. Holy shit, I'm alive!

"Caine!" she shouted, struggling to take off the helmet. "Caine!" Finally, she managed the release and threw the heavy black lifesaver aside. She crawled out of the ditch wet and bruised, her ears ringing, but so very fucking alive. "Caine!" she cried, adrenaline propelling her back to the road.

She pushed onto her knees. *There!* A few feet farther away. Face down at the top edge of the ditch.

"Caine!" She ran and fell at his side. Blood poured from gravel-lined gashes in his cheekbone and his forehead just above his temple. "Caine, can you hear me?"

A single groan. But it was the sweetest, most hopeful thing she'd ever heard.

Until the SUV that'd chased them came to a skidding stop a few feet away.

* * * *

Boots hit the asphalt, and then a tall, thin figure stepped out from behind the driver's door. He wore a ski mask with cut-outs only for his eyes and mouth. The same one from the night he'd tried to grab her.

Bile hit the back of Emma's throat. She couldn't believe that it was all coming down to this.

"Hello, Emma," he said.

Recognition skittered down her spine, but her heart beat too hard and her head hurt too much to pinpoint it. "Who are you? Why are you doing this?"

"I was trying to save you, not hurt you. You weren't supposed to get on the bike." He *ts*ked. "That was his punishment, not yours."

She shook her head, his words not making sense. "I don't understand."

"No, ma'am. I know you don't. But you will." He pulled off the mask, and there stood before her Mr. Wilkerson. The friendly new janitor from school who'd helped her so many times this year.

She blinked once, twice, her brain refusing what was right before her eyes. "Mr. Wilkerson?"

He smiled, like he was pleased she recognized him. "Yes, ma'am. Finally."

She recoiled. "Why are you trying to hurt me?"

His expression went grave and he shook his head. "No, Emma, no. You have it all wrong. I want to keep you safe *always*." He glared at Caine. "And I've already forgiven what you did with that...degenerate. We'll not speak of it again."

What the ever-living hell? How does he know anything? "Um, Mr. Wilkerson, can you just give me a minute to get my breath? I just feel like I need to catch up," she said, slipping as much pleasantry into her voice as she could manage.

"I'm afraid not. At least, not here. Cops are coming. I need you to get in the truck now." When he gestured at the rear door near to him, she realized the hand he pointed with held a gun.

Which was the moment she *finally freaking remembered* that Caine had given her his.

"Okay, okay, Mr. Wilkerson. Just give me a second. I'm a little dizzy," she said, slowly forcing herself to her feet between Caine and the SUV with the pocket that held the gun facing the field. She hoped the oversized bulk of it would shield her hand just long enough.

Sirens. *Way* distant. They might as well have been a hundred miles away, assuming they were coming for them at all. Would they be able to track Caine's 9-1-1 call? She didn't know.

"Hurry, Emma," Wilkerson said, the hard edge of impatience slipping into his tone.

"Okay, okay," she said, pulling the handgun up into the long sleeve. Gingerly, she moved closer to the SUV, then alongside it, but not yet close enough for him to force her in.

"Now, *girl*." All pretense of that slow politeness dropped away.

Caine stirred. His boot twitched. He groaned louder and tried to pull his knee up under him.

"You can't have her ever again," the man growled, going closer and raising the gun. Fully prepared to shoot an injured, unarmed man point blank in the back.

She raised her own gun. "Drop it. *Now*." Even though she'd held and shot a gun before, her hand shook. There was no comparison between pointing at a target and at another human being.

He noticed, his gaze latching onto how the handgun quivered. "Your fucking another man is as much poor behavior as I can take from you, Emma. I can't believe you're going to make me discipline you on our very first night."

"Drop it!" she yelled.

His hand moved. She didn't know if he was preparing to fire at Caine or turn the piece on her. She didn't wait to know. She pulled the trigger. Once, twice, three times, more.

Despite their proximity, it took several shots before she hit him where it counted enough that he finally went down.

But he *did* go down. She approached him like he was a snake that would strike again, and she kicked his gun away from his reach.

Bleary, hateful eyes glared up at her. "Such a disappointment, after all my...work."

She raised the gun again. A hundred percent prepared to shoot and end this once and for all. But then a terrible gurgling sounded out from his throat, and he fell eerily quiet, utterly still.

Stunned and shaky, Emma went to the ground at Caine's side again. Unfocused icy blue eyes swam up at her, and then he attempted to roll to his side, but couldn't quite manage it. But that was enough to make her clutch his hand and squeeze it tight—and say everything she should have said sooner. "Thank God, Caine. Please be okay, baby. Please be okay so I can tell you how sorry I am and how much I love you."

Slow blinks were her only response.

And then sirens bore down on them. Cars skidded to a stop. Voices yelled. Weapons waved. Emma threw away her gun and held up her hands. "Help us," she cried. "He's hurt."

Chaos descended. Cops wanted to talk to her. Paramedics wanted to examine her. Other Raven Riders asked what'd happened.

But all Emma wanted was to get back to Caine. And make sure he was okay.

Chapter 16

Caine came awake on a hard gasp and found his chest and hips strapped down. He fought the restraints like a motherfucker—because they were keeping him from finding Emma.

"Emma!" he shouted. "Emma!" *God, please let her have survived this. Please let her still be here. Please let me have kept my promise, just this one time.* "*Emma!*"

Hands pinned his arms.

And then a face loomed over his. "Caine, stop. Stop, man. It's us. Emma's here. They're checking her out." Dare. It was Dare.

"She's..."

He nodded. "Banged up but good."

"Fuck, *fuck*, her stalker is after us! Let me...*up*," he growled.

"He's gone. It's over," Dare said.

Suddenly Caine was free. Up. On his feet and searching for the threat. But the road tilted and he landed against somebody's chest. Hands held him upright.

"Sir, we need to finish examining you," a voice called.

"I got him," Dare said. "If you can get Emma over here this will get a lot easier."

"Emma," Caine said, his gut roiling with the fear that he'd failed again. He wouldn't survive it. He wouldn't want to. His hands fisted in Dare's cut. "I gotta protect her."

"She's coming. Just slow your roll and get your wits about you. You took a bit of a header and redecorated the ground with a little skin. You don't want to worry her, right?"

Caine nodded, the words slowly but surely making sense. As if parts of him were coming back online one system at a time.

"You should know," Dare said, nailing him with a stare. "She's the one who took the guy out."

He hadn't even processed that when something else demanded his attention more.

"Caine!" The voice was like a magnet. He turned and he and Emma were in each other's arms. "Caine," she moaned, shoulders shaking.

"Oh, sweetness, are you okay?" he asked, his hands running all over her. Making sure she was really real. It was hard as hell to break their connection, but he held her back from him, needing to know. Needing to *see*. And, aw, God, she was beautiful. Dirt on her face and hair a mess and angry-looking road burn on her chin. Beautiful.

Her hands cupped his neck. "I'm okay. I'm okay, Caine. All because of you. You saved me…"

"Christ, I'm sorry you had to be the one to end this," he said, hating that she'd forever have that memory. He knew firsthand how such things could eat at you in the dark of night.

"I'm not," she rasped, those blue eyes so bright with life. "And we ended it together, Caine. But how are you? I was so scared. You wouldn't wake up at first."

He pulled her into his arms, needing her heat against him more than he needed his next breath. "I'm fine. But, oh, fuck, I'm *not* fine. I'm so goddamn sorry." His voice cracked as he suddenly remembered everything that led up to the crash. "I didn't mean to hurt you. I *never* want to hurt you. Can you ever forgive—"

Emma kissed him. Her tongue in his mouth. Her arms around his neck. Her body pressed tight. It was forgiveness and acceptance in a physical act, and he felt it into his very soul.

Deep and slow, he kissed her back for everything he was worth. And for the first time, he actually believed he was worth *something*. To her. His injuries faded. The people disappeared. And they were alone and safe.

"Did you hear me before?" she asked when she pulled back from the kiss. Her eyes were blue fire looking at him, looking into the very depths of him.

"I…I don't know."

She rested her forehead against his. "Then let me tell you again. *I love you*. Every bit of you. Your past and your present and your mistakes and your strengths. I love you, Caine. Nothing else matters to me. And trust me, I've considered it all."

A sob ripped up his throat. His arms went around her and he pressed his mouth to her hair. "I...*Christ*...I fucking love you, too. I wasn't sure I knew what it was, Emma. Or maybe I didn't believe I was capable of it. But I came awake and you weren't there and in that moment I knew my whole world began and ended with you."

They fell into each other again, but suddenly there was a mob around them.

"When did all these people get here?" Caine asked.

"He really needs to be seen," a paramedic argued. And was that Dare's voice? Phoenix's? Everything was too much for Caine to make sense of it.

"We'll go," Emma was saying. "We'll both go. But only if you can transport us in the same ambulance."

Caine pulled Emma into his chest, not caring in the slightest that he suddenly felt about two dozen bruises all down his front. Or that all these people might've heard their words. Funny how nearly losing the most important thing in your life suddenly made what mattered most so fucking clear. And that was her. Them. Together.

Caine nodded. "What she said. Because no one's ever separating us again."

* * * *

Five Weeks Later

"I protest you going back to work," Caine said, tempting Emma to stay right there in their bed where they'd spent so much of the past month. After the accident and the investigation into the stalking, she'd taken a leave of absence that was now coming to an end. And she regretted it, too.

She chuckled and pressed a kiss to his shoulder. The one with ink covering scars. God, he was so beautiful. "No one will pay me to stay in bed all day."

He reached for his wallet on the nightstand, the stretch making him groan just a little. Neither of them had broken anything, and both were nearly fully healed up, but it was amazing how long a body continued to feel a head-on collision with the large immovable object known as the ground. He counted bills out onto his naked chest. "I got sixty-seven dollars. How much more time will that get me?"

Emma laughed, absolutely in love with this new silly side. And his hopeful side. And the side of him that looked toward the future—and saw himself there. Really, she just loved all of him.

Some of his newfound—and hard-fought—optimism was having the threat behind them—Caine knew more about it than Emma did. She didn't want to hide from the truth, but her psyche didn't need all the disturbing details, either. What she'd been willing to learn was that Wilkerson had targeted her from almost his first day at Frederick Elementary, judging by time stamps on photos and videos they found on his phone. But now that was all over. And Emma had quickly been cleared of any wrongdoing in his death.

Some of it was the way they'd opened up to each other in the wake of nearly losing everything. Shooting Wilkerson was something she'd remember forever. Taking a life wasn't a memory she liked having, but it also wasn't something she regretted. Not given the circumstances. And it gave her a whole new understanding of the shooting Caine had described to her. She couldn't blame him for it, not when Emma would've shot her attacker again even after she'd disarmed him. It was a terrible thing to know about herself, but it was true. And they didn't hide from the truth.

For Caine's part, opening up had meant that he had to face the trauma he'd endured. He had to walk through the terrible messy pain of it. It'd taken him four introductory appointments before he found someone he thought he could actually talk to, but he had found someone, and he was going to therapy. And that was huge.

"Dude, I'm sorry, but sixty-seven dollars is *not* enough for all this." She slipped out of bed and strutted her nakedness to the door. If she didn't get in the shower soon, she was going to see her kindergartners again smelling like two hours of sex.

"What about this, then?"

The oddness of his voice made her lean back in the doorway. "What?"

Caine was getting on his knees by their bed. Also totally naked. He held a blue velvet box in his hand that he opened while she watched.

"Caine," she gasped, the room spinning around her.

"Marry me," he said, those odd, pale eyes nearly glowing. "You're so fucking perfect for me, and you have been since the first moment we met. You're already my everything, Emma. So marry me."

She went to her knees in front of him, and thought it was *perfection* that they were both bare in this moment. "Anything, Caine. Everything. You know I want it all with you. I'll marry you. How could I not when I love you so much?"

He slipped the ring on, a commitment to always be there for each other. To always believe. To always try.

A commitment they made every one of the many days, months, and years that followed after that. Years that included Emma finishing her graduate degree, Caine becoming a regular volunteer at the LGBT youth center they'd donated to that first Christmas, and a baby girl with Emma's blond hair and Caine's pale eyes. A daughter they named Grace.

* * * *

Also from 1001 Dark Nights and Laura Kaye, discover Hard As Steel, Hard To Serve, and Eyes On You.

A Note from the Author

In *Ride Dirty*, Emma shares her new Christmas Day tradition of choosing a child-related charity to support. Her possible choices so align with Caine's own experiences that he's blindsided by unexpected emotion. That scene was incredibly emotional for me to write, and the depth of my own reaction surprised me, too. But it's easy to know why—in researching which charities Emma might give to, I immersed myself in the experiences of the children who desperately need these organizations. And that got me right in the heart.

If you would like more information about or would like to donate to organizations like CASA and the LGBTQ center/shelter that they discuss, here are a few to consider. Of course, there are similar organizations that need your help in communities around the country—no doubt including yours. I encourage you to look, donate, and volunteer locally, too.

National CASA (Court Appointed Special Advocates) http://www.casaforchildren.org/

Maryland CASA (where the series is set) http://marylandcasa.org/

True Colors Fund https://truecolorsfund.org/ - Mission: to end homelessness among lesbian, gay, bisexual, and transgender youth, creating a world where all young people can be their true selves.

The Ali Forney Center, New York City https://www.aliforneycenter.org/ - Mission: to protect LGBTQ youths from the harms of homelessness and empower them with the tools needed to live independently

The Trevor Project (LGBT crisis intervention and suicide prevention) https://www.thetrevorproject.org/

Sign up for the 1001 Dark Nights Newsletter
and be entered to win a Tiffany Key necklace.

There's a contest every month!

Go to www.1001DarkNights.com to subscribe.

As a bonus, all subscribers will receive a free copy of
Discovery Bundle Three
Featuring stories by
Sidney Bristol, Darcy Burke, T. Gephart
Stacey Kennedy, Adriana Locke
JB Salsbury, and Erika Wilde

Discover 1001 Dark Nights Collection Five
Go to www.1001DarkNights.com to explore.

BLAZE ERUPTING by Rebecca Zanetti
Scorpius Syndrome/A Brigade Novella

ROUGH RIDE by Kristen Ashley
A Chaos Novella

HAWKYN by Larissa Ione
A Demonica Underworld Novella

RIDE DIRTY by Laura Kaye
A Raven Riders Novella

ROME'S CHANCE by Joanna Wylde
A Reapers MC Novella

THE MARRIAGE ARRANGEMENT by Jennifer Probst
A Marriage to a Billionaire Novella

SURRENDER by Elisabeth Naughton
A House of Sin Novella

INKED NIGHT by Carrie Ann Ryan
A Montgomery Ink Novella

ENVY by Rachel Van Dyken
An Eagle Elite Novella

PROTECTED by Lexi Blake
A Masters and Mercenaries Novella

THE PRINCE by Jennifer L. Armentrout
A Wicked Novella

PLEASE ME by J. Kenner
A Stark Ever After Novella

WOUND TIGHT by Lorelei James
A Rough Riders/Blacktop Cowboys Novella®

STRONG by Kylie Scott
A Stage Dive Novella

DRAGON NIGHT by Donna Grant
A Dark Kings Novella

TEMPTING BROOKE by Kristen Proby
A Big Sky Novella

HAUNTED BE THE HOLIDAYS by Heather Graham
A Krewe of Hunters Novella

CONTROL by K. Bromberg
An Everyday Heroes Novella

HUNKY HEARTBREAKER by Kendall Ryan
A Whiskey Kisses Novella

THE DARKEST CAPTIVE by Gena Showalter
A Lords of the Underworld Novella

Discover 1001 Dark Nights Collection One
Go to www.1001DarkNights.com to explore.

FOREVER WICKED by Shayla Black
CRIMSON TWILIGHT by Heather Graham
CAPTURED IN SURRENDER by Liliana Hart
SILENT BITE: A SCANGUARDS WEDDING by Tina Folsom
DUNGEON GAMES by Lexi Blake
AZAGOTH by Larissa Ione
NEED YOU NOW by Lisa Renee Jones
SHOW ME, BABY by Cherise Sinclair
ROPED IN by Lorelei James
TEMPTED BY MIDNIGHT by Lara Adrian
THE FLAME by Christopher Rice
CARESS OF DARKNESS by Julie Kenner

Also from 1001 Dark Nights

TAME ME by J. Kenner

Discover 1001 Dark Nights Collection Two

Go to www.1001DarkNights.com to explore.

WICKED WOLF by Carrie Ann Ryan
WHEN IRISH EYES ARE HAUNTING by Heather Graham
EASY WITH YOU by Kristen Proby
MASTER OF FREEDOM by Cherise Sinclair
CARESS OF PLEASURE by Julie Kenner
ADORED by Lexi Blake
HADES by Larissa Ione
RAVAGED by Elisabeth Naughton
DREAM OF YOU by Jennifer L. Armentrout
STRIPPED DOWN by Lorelei James
RAGE/KILLIAN by Alexandra Ivy/Laura Wright
DRAGON KING by Donna Grant
PURE WICKED by Shayla Black
HARD AS STEEL by Laura Kaye
STROKE OF MIDNIGHT by Lara Adrian
ALL HALLOWS EVE by Heather Graham
KISS THE FLAME by Christopher Rice
DARING HER LOVE by Melissa Foster
TEASED by Rebecca Zanetti
THE PROMISE OF SURRENDER by Liliana Hart

Also from 1001 Dark Nights

THE SURRENDER GATE By Christopher Rice
SERVICING THE TARGET By Cherise Sinclair

Discover 1001 Dark Nights Collection Three

Go to www.1001DarkNights.com to explore.

HIDDEN INK by Carrie Ann Ryan
BLOOD ON THE BAYOU by Heather Graham
SEARCHING FOR MINE by Jennifer Probst
DANCE OF DESIRE by Christopher Rice
ROUGH RHYTHM by Tessa Bailey
DEVOTED by Lexi Blake
Z by Larissa Ione
FALLING UNDER YOU by Laurelin Paige
EASY FOR KEEPS by Kristen Proby
UNCHAINED by Elisabeth Naughton
HARD TO SERVE by Laura Kaye
DRAGON FEVER by Donna Grant
KAYDEN/SIMON by Alexandra Ivy/Laura Wright
STRUNG UP by Lorelei James
MIDNIGHT UNTAMED by Lara Adrian
TRICKED by Rebecca Zanetti
DIRTY WICKED by Shayla Black
THE ONLY ONE by Lauren Blakely
SWEET SURRENDER by Liliana Hart

Discover 1001 Dark Nights Collection Four

Go to www.1001DarkNights.com to explore.

ROCK CHICK REAWAKENING by Kristen Ashley
ADORING INK by Carrie Ann Ryan
SWEET RIVALRY by K. Bromberg
SHADE'S LADY by Joanna Wylde
RAZR by Larissa Ione
ARRANGED by Lexi Blake
TANGLED by Rebecca Zanetti
HOLD ME by J. Kenner
SOMEHOW, SOME WAY by Jennifer Probst
TOO CLOSE TO CALL by Tessa Bailey
HUNTED by Elisabeth Naughton
EYES ON YOU by Laura Kaye
BLADE by Alexandra Ivy/Laura Wright
DRAGON BURN by Donna Grant
TRIPPED OUT by Lorelei James
STUD FINDER by Lauren Blakely
MIDNIGHT UNLEASHED by Lara Adrian
HALLOW BE THE HAUNT by Heather Graham
DIRTY FILTHY FIX by Laurelin Paige
THE BED MATE by Kendall Ryan
PRINCE ROMAN by CD Reiss
NO RESERVATIONS by Kristen Proby
DAWN OF SURRENDER by Liliana Hart

Also from 1001 Dark Nights

Tempt Me by J. Kenner

About Laura Kaye

Laura is the New York Times and USA Today bestselling author of over thirty books in contemporary and erotic romance and romantic suspense, including the Raven Riders, Blasphemy, and Hard Ink series. Growing up, Laura's large extended family believed in the supernatural, and family lore involving angels, ghosts, and evil-eye curses cemented in Laura a life-long fascination with storytelling and all things paranormal. Laura also writes historical fiction as the NYT bestselling author Laura Kamoie. She lives in Maryland with her husband and two daughters, and appreciates her view of the Chesapeake Bay every day.

Learn more at www.LauraKayeAuthor.com

Join Laura's Newsletter for Exclusives & Giveaways!

Fighting For Everything
Warrior Fight Club #1
By Laura Kaye
Coming May 22, 2018

Loving her is the biggest fight of his life…

Home from the Marines, Noah Cortez has a secret he doesn't want his oldest friend, Kristina Moore, to know. It kills him to push her away, especially when he's noticing just how sexy and confident she's become in his absence. But, angry and full of fight, he's not the same man anymore either. Which is why Warrior Fight Club sounds so good.

Kristina loves teaching, but she wants more out of life. She wants Noah—the boy she's crushed on and waited for. Except Noah is all man now—in ways both oh so good and troubling, too. Still, she wants who he's become—every war-hardened inch. And when they finally stop fighting their attraction, it's everything Kristina never dared hope for.

But Noah is secretly spiraling, and when he lashes out, it threatens what he and Kristina have found. The brotherhood of the fight club helps him confront his demons, but only Noah can convince the woman he loves that he's finally ready to fight for everything.

* * * *

Noah had really gone and done it now, hadn't he? Opened his mouth and spewed his poison at one of the most important people in his life. And tonight was supposed to be all about making amends.

Goddamnit, the minute he came out of that flashback he should've gotten the hell away from her. He'd just been so shell-shocked by how realistic it had seemed. The anti-aircraft fire. The crashing Blackhawk. The screaming chaos. He'd been even more stunned that Kristina had kissed him to pull him back—and that it had worked.

He shook his head, ignoring the fuck out of the wave of dizziness that threatened, and grabbed the doorknob. "I'm sorry. I'll go."

"*No*," she said, her voice stern. Frowning, he dragged his gaze to her to see her fingers working at the knot in her dress's belt. She pulled it apart and let the fabric fall. The dress swung open, baring her all down the front. "You need me. Have me."

He blinked, once, twice, and his jaw fell open.

Jesus. She was beautiful, gorgeous, a fucking fantasy of soft, feminine curves. His pulse beat so hard he could feel it beneath his skin. Everywhere.

Noah gripped the doorknob harder, anchoring him in the moment. Keeping him from taking something that wasn't his to take. No matter how much he might want it. "Kris—"

"Have me, Noah." She shrugged the dress off her shoulders. It fell to the floor in a soft rush, leaving Kristina standing there in a pair of strappy silver sandals and a matching pale blue and white satin bra-and-panty set.

He couldn't do this. Not to her, not to them. But his brain seemed to be the only part of him riding the do-the-right-thing train. Because his heart *wanted*. And his cock fucking *needed*. He licked his lips and shook his head, feeling solid ground slide out from beneath his feet with every breath. "I'm a fucking wreck, Kristina."

"Then be *my* fucking wreck." She shrugged and shifted her feet, and Noah studied these small movements, trying to decipher what they meant. "Just for tonight."

"Just for tonight?" He tried out the words—and their meaning. Could he really let himself have her...just this once? The idea that he could escape all the bullshit in his head—just for one night, the idea that he could work out this crazy desire for her...and maybe get it out of his system. It was all so damn tempting. *She* was so damn tempting. When had that happened? Why was he seeing her so differently? And did any of that even matter? "I don't want to use you," he said, his thoughts flying and tearing him in two.

She stepped closer. Heat flashed over Noah's skin. God, she was brave. So much braver than him. "You wouldn't," Kristina said. "Because I...I *want* you to fuck me, Noah. You think you're the only one dreaming of that? Imagining it? Fantasizing about it? I wake up from those dreams and you're not there...and it *hurts*. It feels like there's a fire inside me that only you can cool. So maybe, maybe if we do this, if we give in, just this once..."

Her words resonated inside him, so deep it was like she was speaking his mind. "What?" he asked, his heart a runaway train in his chest.

"Maybe it will get rid of this tension between us." She hugged herself, plumping those beautiful breasts and making waves of soft blond fall around her shoulders.

He let go of the doorknob, but forced his feet to remain planted right where they were. Because if he got any closer to her, his brain was going to be off the hook for the rest of the night. "So this would be...just sex?" he asked, his chest rising and falling heavily.

Nodding, she looked him right in the eye. "Just sex. Just this one night."

He swallowed. Hard. He was so damn hungry for her, and that made him hesitate when all he wanted to do was give in. "I'm strung so tight right now, Kristina. I don't know if I can be gentle." He shook his head and forced his fists to unclench, but aggression was a living beast within him. "That wouldn't be right. That wouldn't be—"

"I don't want gentle, Noah." The smile she gave him was so confident, so sexy. When had she become so goddamned amazing? Or had she always been? "I just want you, however you are."

One second he was standing at the door, the next he was all over her. Hands in her hair, forcing her head back and her mouth open to him. Lips sliding over hers, claiming, sucking, tongue penetrating. Body fused to hers, pushing her back, one stumbling step after another, and trying to get closer. And closer. And closer.

"Oh God," Kristina moaned, her hands clutching at his neck, his shoulders, his hair.

"One night," he said, lifting her and wrapping her thighs around his hips. Her ass felt so lush in his hands he couldn't help squeezing.

"One night. I need you. Now. Here. Anywhere."

Sucking and licking at her throat, he stalked down the hall toward her bedroom. "No. I want you under me." In her room, he went right for her big bed with all its pretty blue and yellow covers and pillows. Standing beside the bed, he laid her out, the weight of his upper body coming down on top of her and making him grind right against the delicious heat between her legs.

"Oh, yes," Kristina said, her hips thrusting against his.

Nearly frantic, he fumbled at the buttons to his jeans. "Need in you."

"Yeah."

"Promise I'll take care of you." He shoved his jeans down around his thighs, freeing his cock against the satin of her panties.

Kristina moaned. "I know you will."

"Fuck, need you. Need you so much." He tugged her panties off, then took himself in hand. Standing between her spread thighs, he rubbed his head against her entrance, feeling her wetness, spreading it around. He wished he could go slower, savor, linger. She braced her feet against the edge of the bed and pushed, trying to impale herself on him. "Shit. Condom," he said. Resisting the urge to plunge forward was almost painful.

"On birth control. Now, Noah."

On a groan, he was inside her, sinking deep, finding home. Fucking hot and tight and perfect. And then he was all the way there, buried deep, as deep as he could go. Just like he'd been yearning for. Only the reality was worlds better than anything his imagination had been able to conjure. It was so good it sent him flying.

He came down over her as much as the position allowed, his hands curling around her shoulders.

She cried out, her hands clawing at his back. "Holy shit, you're big."

"You okay?" he asked, the comment making his balls heavy and sending an urgent demand to move down his spine.

"So much more than okay," Kristina said in a breathy, awed voice.

"Then hold on."

Discover More Laura Kaye

Eyes On You
A Blasphemy Novella

She wants to explore her true desires, and he wants to watch…

When a sexy stranger asks Wolf Henrikson to rescue her from a bad date, he never expected to want the woman for himself. But their playful conversation turns into a scorching one-night stand that reveals the shy beauty gets off on the idea of being seen, even if she's a little scared of it, too. And Wolf loves to watch.

In the wake of discovering her fiancé's infidelity, florist Olivia Foster never expected to find someone who not only understood her wildest, darkest fantasies, but would bring them to life. As Wolf introduces her to his world at the play club, Blasphemy, Liv finds herself tempted to explore submission and exhibitionism with the hard-bodied Dom even as she's scared to trust again.

But Wolf is a master of getting what he wants—and he's got his eyes set on her…

* * * *

Hard As Steel
A Hard Ink/Raven Riders Crossover

After identifying her employer's dangerous enemies, Jessica Jakes takes refuge at the compound of the Raven Riders Motorcycle Club. Fellow Hard Ink tattooist and Raven leader Ike Young promises to keep Jess safe for as long as it takes, which would be perfect if his close, personal, round-the-clock protection didn't make it so hard to hide just how much she wants him--and always has.

Ike Young loved and lost a woman in trouble once before. The last thing he needs is alone time with the sexiest and feistiest woman he's ever known, one he's purposely kept at a distance for years. Now, Ike's not sure he can keep his hands or his heart to himself--or that he even wants to anymore. And that means he has to do whatever it takes to hold on to Jess forever.

* * * *

Hard To Serve
A Hard Ink Novella

To protect and serve is all Detective Kyler Vance ever wanted to do, so when Internal Affairs investigates him as part of the new police commissioner's bid to oust corruption, everything is on the line. Which makes meeting a smart, gorgeous submissive at an exclusive play club the perfect distraction...

The director of the city's hottest art gallery, Mia Breslin's career is golden. Now if only she could find a man to dominate her nights and set her body—and her heart—on fire. When a scorching scene with a hard-bodied, brooding Dom at Blasphemy promises just that, Mia is lured to serve Kyler again and again.

Then, as their relationship burns hotter, Kyler learns that he's been dominating the daughter of the hard-ass boss who has it in for him. Now Kyler must choose between life-long duty and forbidden desire before Mia finds another who's not so hard to serve.

On behalf of 1001 Dark Nights,

Liz Berry and M.J. Rose would like to thank ~

Steve Berry
Doug Scofield
Kim Guidroz
Jillian Stein
InkSlinger PR
Dan Slater
Asha Hossain
Chris Graham
Fedora Chen
Kasi Alexander
Jessica Johns
Dylan Stockton
Richard Blake
BookTrib After Dark
and Simon Lipskar

71229150R00105

Made in the USA
San Bernardino, CA
13 March 2018